JUNIOR DRUG AWARENESS

How to Say No to Drugs

JUNIOR DRUG AWARENESS

Alcohol

Amphetamines and
Other Stimulants

Cocaine and Crack

Diet Pills

Ecstasy and Other Club Drugs

Heroin

How to Say No to Drugs

Inhalants and Solvents

Marijuana

Nicotine

Over-the-Counter Drugs

Prozac and Other
Antidepressants

Steroids and Other
Performance-Enhancing
Drugs

Vicodin, OxyContin, and
Other Pain Relievers

JUNIOR DRUG AWARENESS

How to Say No to Drugs

Damian P. Kreske

CHELSEA HOUSE
PUBLISHERS
An imprint of Infobase Publishing

Junior Drug Awareness: How to Say No to Drugs
Copyright © 2008 by Infobase Publishing

Chelsea House
An imprint of Infobase Publishing
132 West 31st Street
New York NY 10001

Library of Congress Cataloging-in-Publication Data

Kreske, Damian P.
  How to say no to drugs / Damian P. Kreske.
      p. cm. — (Junior drug awareness)
  Includes bibliographical references and index.
  ISBN 978-0-7910-9699-4 (hardcover)
  1. Drug abuse—Juvenile literature. I. Title.

  HV5809.5.K745 2008
  613.8—dc22   2007043664

Chelsea House books are available at special discounts when purchased in bulk quantities for businesses, associations, institutions, or sales promotions. Please call our Special Sales Department in New York at (212) 967-8800 or (800) 322-8755.

You can find Chelsea House on the World Wide Web
at http://www.chelseahouse.com

Text design by Erik Lindstrom
Cover design by Jooyoung An

Printed in the United States

Bang NMSG 10 9 8 7 6 5 4 3 2 1

This book is printed on acid-free paper.

All links and web addresses were checked and verified to be correct at the time of publication. Because of the dynamic nature of the web, some addresses and links may have changed since publication and may no longer be valid.

CONTENTS

INTRODUCTION
Battling a Pandemic: A History of Drugs
in the United States   6
by Ronald J. Brogan,
Regional Director of D.A.R.E. America

1   Are Drugs Helpful or Harmful?   12

2   Drugs in Popular Culture   24

3   Where to Learn About Drugs   37

4   Commonly Abused Legal Drugs   47

5   Illegal Drugs That Are Abused   59

**6   How Drugs Affect Users, Family,
       and Friends**   73

7   How to Handle Drug Use and Abuse   83

       Glossary   94

       Bibliography   97

       Further Reading   107

       Picture Credits   108

       Index   109

       About the Authors   112

Battling a Pandemic: A History of Drugs in the United States

When Johnny came marching home again after the Civil War, he probably wasn't marching in a very straight line. This is because Johnny, like 400,000 of his fellow drug-addled soldiers, was addicted to morphine. With the advent of morphine and the invention of the hypodermic needle, drug addiction became a prominent problem during the nineteenth century. It was the first time such widespread drug dependency was documented in history.

Things didn't get much better in the later decades of the nineteenth century. Cocaine and opiates were used as over-the-counter "medicines." Of course, the most famous was Coca-Cola, which actually did contain cocaine in its early days.

6

After the turn of the twentieth century, drug abuse was spiraling out of control, and the United States government stepped in with the first regulatory controls. In 1906, the Pure Food and Drug Act became a law. It required the labeling of product ingredients. Next came the Harrison Narcotics Tax Act of 1914, which outlawed illegal importation or distribution of cocaine and opiates. During this time, neither the medical community nor the general population was aware of the principles of addiction.

After the passage of the Harrison Act, drug addiction was not a major issue in the United States until the 1960s, when drug abuse became a much bigger social problem. During this time, the federal government's drug enforcement agencies were found to be ineffective. Organizations often worked against one another, causing counterproductive effects. By 1973, things had gotten so bad that President Richard Nixon, by executive order, created the Drug Enforcement Administration (DEA), which became the lead agency in all federal narcotics investigations. It continues in that role to this day. The effectiveness of enforcement and the so-called "Drug War" are open to debate. Cocaine use has been reduced by 75% since its peak in 1985. However, its replacement might be methamphetamine (speed, crank, crystal), which is arguably more dangerous and is now plaguing the country. Also, illicit drugs tend to be cyclical; various drugs, such as LSD, seem to appear, disappear, and then reappear again. It is probably closest to the truth to say that a war on drugs can never be won, just managed.

Fighting drugs involves a three-pronged battle. Enforcement is one prong. Education and prevention is the second. Treatment is the third.

Although pandemics of drug abuse have been with us for more than 150 years, education and prevention were not seriously considered until the 1970s. In 1982, former First Lady Betty Ford made drug treatment socially acceptable with the opening of the Betty Ford Center. This followed her own battle with addiction. Other treatment centers—including Hazelton, Fair Oaks, and Smithers (now called the Addiction Institute of New York)—added to the growing number of clinics, and soon detox facilities were in almost every city. The cost of a single day in one of these facilities is often more than $1,000, and the effectiveness of treatment centers is often debated. To this day, there is little regulation over who can practice counseling.

It soon became apparent that the most effective way to deal with the drug problem was prevention by education. By some estimates, the overall cost of drug abuse to society exceeds $250 billion per year; preventive education is certainly the most cost-effective way to deal with the problem. Drug education can save people from misery, pain, and ultimately even jail time or death. In the early 1980s, First Lady Nancy Reagan started the "Just Say No" program. Although many scoffed at the program, its promotion of total abstinence from drugs has been effective with many adolescents. In the late 1980s, drug education was not science-based, and people essentially were throwing mud at the wall to see what would stick. Motivations of all types spawned hundreds, if not thousands, of drug-education programs. Promoters of some programs used whatever political clout they could muster to get on various government agencies' lists of most effective programs. The bottom line, however, is that prevention is very difficult to quantify. It's nearly impossible to prove that drug use would have occurred if it were not prevented from happening.

In 1983, the Los Angeles Unified School District, in conjunction with the Los Angeles Police Department, started what was considered at that time to be the gold standard of school-based drug education pro- grams. The program was called Drug Abuse Resistance Education, otherwise known as D.A.R.E. The program called for specially trained police officers to deliver drug-education programs in schools. This was an era in which community-oriented policing was all the rage. The logic was that kids would give street credibility to a police officer who spoke to them about drugs. The popularity of the program was unprecedented. It spread all across the country and around the world. Ultimately, 80% of American school districts would utilize the program. Parents, police officers, and kids all loved it. Unexpectedly, a special bond was formed between the kids who took the program and the police officers who ran it. Even in adulthood, many kids remember the name of their D.A.R.E. officer.

By 1991, national drug use had been halved. In any other medical-oriented field, this figure would be aston- ishing. The number of people in the United States using drugs went from about 25 million in the early 1980s to 11 million in 1991. All three prongs of the battle against drugs vied for government dollars, with each prong claiming credit for the reduction in drug use. There is no doubt that each contributed to the decline in drug use, but most people agreed that preventing drug abuse before it started had proved to be the most effective strategy. The National Institute on Drug Abuse (NIDA), which was established in 1974, defines its mandate in this way: "NIDA's mission is to lead the Nation in bring- ing the power of science to bear on drug abuse and addiction." NIDA leaders were the experts in prevention and treatment, and they had enormous resources. In

1986, the nonprofit Partnership for a Drug-Free America was founded. The organization defined its mission as, "Putting to use all major media outlets, including TV, radio, print advertisements and the Internet, along with the pro bono work of the country's best advertising agencies." The Partnership for a Drug-Free America is responsible for the popular campaign that compared "your brain on drugs" to fried eggs.

The American drug problem was front-page news for years up until 1990–1991. Then the Gulf War took over the news, and drugs never again regained the headlines. Most likely, this lack of media coverage has led to some peaks and valleys in the number of people using drugs, but there has not been a return to anything near the high percentage of use recorded in 1985. According to the University of Michigan's 2006 Monitoring the Future study, which measured adolescent drug use, there were 840,000 fewer American kids using drugs in 2006 than in 2001. This represents a 23% reduction in drug use. With the exception of prescription drugs, drug use continues to decline.

In 2000, the Robert Wood Johnson Foundation recognized that the D.A.R.E. Program, with its tens of thousands of trained police officers, had the top state-of-the-art delivery system of drug education in the world. The foundation dedicated $15 million to develop a cutting-edge prevention curriculum to be delivered by D.A.R.E. The new D.A.R.E. program incorporates the latest in prevention and education, including high-tech, interactive, and decision-model-based approaches. D.A.R.E. officers are trained as "coaches" who support kids as they practice research-based refusal strategies in high-stakes peer-pressure environments. Through stunning magnetic resonance imaging (MRI) images, students get to see tangible proof of how various substances diminish brain activity.

Will this program be the solution to the drug problem in the United States? By itself, probably not. It is simply an integral part of a larger equation that everyone involved hopes will prevent kids from ever starting to use drugs. The equation also requires guidance in the home, without which no program can be effective.

Ronald J. Brogan
Regional Director
D.A.R.E America

1

Are Drugs Helpful or Harmful?

People use the word *drug* to mean many different things. Doctors tell their patients to take certain drugs to heal health problems. But then you might hear teachers and parents telling you to say no to drugs. And then your friends might talk about drugs that they have heard about from other people, seen on TV, or heard in a song. What one source says about drugs might be very different than what another source says. It can be confusing to sort out all of this information.

DRUGS THAT HELP, DRUGS THAT HURT

It helps to know what a drug is before trying to understand information about different drugs. A drug is a substance that changes how the body works after a person takes it. Drugs come in many sizes and shapes and are used for different purposes. For example, a doctor might give her patient a heart-related medicine—one kind of drug—to help him recover from a heart attack. The doctor gives her patient this drug to change the way his body works in order to improve his health.

Yet, not all drugs are helpful. In a very different example, a person might take **cocaine** to get **high**. This kind of drug use is different from taking a heart-related medicine. Instead of helping a person's health, cocaine and other illegal drugs damage it.

LEGAL VERSUS ILLEGAL DRUGS

Medicines or medications are drugs that are legal and given to someone by a doctor. The doctor gives his patient a certain amount of the drug in order to improve that person's health.

Still, drugs that are legal can harm people when taken incorrectly. Doctors give very specific instructions on how much of the drug should be taken. If someone takes too much of the drug, takes it too often, or mixes it with other drugs, there could be serious health problems as a result. That person could get very sick, or even die. In recent years, more and more people who are not sick have been taking strong medications in order to get high. When improperly used, many medications can be just as dangerous as illegal drugs.

Other legal drugs such as alcohol (in beer, wine, and liquor) and **nicotine** (in cigarettes) can also cause problems, even though they are legal. These drugs can be dangerous if abused and will often lead to **addiction**. Laws have been passed to keep young people under a certain age from buying alcohol and cigarettes. In the United States, a person must be at least 18 years old to

A sick person who takes over-the-counter cold medication and cough syrups may experience temporary relief for their symptoms. However, healthy people abusing these medicines risk harming themselves, especially if they mix the OTC drugs with alcohol or other drugs.

buy cigarettes and at least 21 years old to buy alcohol. The laws attempt to protect young people from the possible hazards of these drugs by banning the use of them altogether.

Drugs that are illegal, such as **heroin** and cocaine, aren't safe to use—ever. Laws have been passed to protect people of all ages from these unsafe substances. If someone breaks the law by using an illegal drug, he or she could go to jail or face other punishments.

The explanation of why some drugs are legal while others are illegal is a complicated issue. The answer depends on many components, including social norms, morality, medical research, and politics. What people consider "normal" for society in terms of the use of drugs is often in line with their **morals**, or personal set of rules about what is right or wrong. Drugs that are

ANIMALS AND INSECTS IN DRUG STORIES

When animals and insects get mixed up with drug users, the stories range from ridiculous to fascinating.

HIGH ON A HORSE

In 2007, a woman was arrested and charged with riding a horse on an Alabama street while intoxicated. She was under the influence of an unspecified **controlled substance** and also in possession of crystal **methamphetamine**, some marijuana, pills, and a pipe. The woman had gotten away from police officers and even rammed a police car with the horse before being taken into custody. She was also charged with cruelty to animals.

FINDING NEW HIGHS

It seems that people are always looking to nature to find new ways to get high. Some studies have been done to test the drug characteristics of the venom of the Sonoran Desert toad. The venom is too toxic to take in by licking the toad, as is often done by people who take toad venom as a drug. Because of this, people have taken to smoking the venom. When smoked, the venom may be less toxic, and is said to cause **hallucinations**.

Another surprising candidate for hallucinogenic effects is the sting of a scorpion found in South Gujarat in India. Supposedly, after the pain of the sting wears off, the user experiences a "floating feeling." The possible results of continued scorpion venom use include kidney failure and heart problems.

(continues on page 16)

(continued from page 15)
DRUG-SNIFFING DOGS AND WASPS
News footage of dogs working with drug officers on U.S. borders is a common sight. These dogs are trained to sniff out drugs that people try to bring into the United States to sell. These dogs are very effective. In 2001, they sniffed out more than a million pounds of marijuana, more than 26,000 pounds of cocaine, and $21.6 million in cash. This resulted in about 8,000 arrests. While this is impressive, it takes many hours—and a lot of money—to train the dogs.

Another idea to find drugs is still being developed: drug-sniffing wasps. In a laboratory, wasps in a container have been trained to smell a particular chemical. When the wasps smell the chemical, they react and move towards the source. Wasps can be trained to do this within 30 minutes. Trained wasps would be a cheaper alternative to using dogs to sniff out drugs, and can be released to the wild after they are used.

sold in the United States typically go through a series of tests by a government agency called the Food and Drug Administration to see if they are safe for public consumption and if they actually work well enough to support the manufacturers' claims.

RECREATIONAL USE OF DRUGS
The use of drugs as a way to unwind, relax, or get high is referred to as "recreational" drug use. People taking

drugs in this way might think using drugs is fun, even though it is often dangerous. The fact is that overusing legal drugs and abusing illegal drugs is not just wrong for health reasons—it's also illegal in most cases.

RECENT TRENDS: NOT EVERYONE SAYS "YES" TO DRUGS

Every year, the Monitoring the Future (MTF) survey asks students in the eighth, tenth, and twelfth grades about their drug use. The 2006 survey shows positive trends among students in the three grades:

- Compared to 2001, 23% fewer students in all three grades said they had used drugs in the past month.
- In every year since 1997, all three grades have reported a decrease in marijuana use.
- Fewer tenth graders—1.8%, down from 2.9%— reported using methamphetamine in the past year. Also, more twelfth graders said they felt crystal methamphetamine was risky to use.
- The recreational use of the pain-reliving medication **OxyContin** has decreased among twelfth-graders. (Eighth- and tenth-graders were not surveyed for this drug.)
- During the past four years, fewer students in all three grades have said they have ever tried a cigarette.
- During the past four years, fewer students in all three grades have reported using alcohol.
- More and more twelfth-graders are realizing that **anabolic steroids** are harmful. (Eighth- and tenth-graders were not asked this question.)

DRUG TESTING IN SCHOOLS

Even though the Monitoring the Future survey has shown a drop in drug use among young people, many studies and surveys show that it is still a problem—and should not be ignored. One idea to combat drug use is to randomly test students for drugs while they attend school.

Some people support the idea, but others believe that randomly testing students for drugs in school goes against the Fourth Amendment. This law, part of the U.S. Constitution, says that police may not search a person's property unless they suspect that person is doing something illegal. A person's "property" also includes his or her body, which means random drug testing falls under the Fourth Amendment. But, in 2002, the U.S. Supreme Court supported drug testing in schools as a way to discourage students from using drugs. Supporters of testing say that students will have an easier time turning down offers of drugs from their peers because they can use school drug testing as their reason. Otherwise, supporters say, students may feel too embarrassed to express their moral or health-related beliefs.

As of 2007, the federal government has given funds to 497 schools nationwide for drug testing. And 500 more schools have tested for drugs without using federal funding. Overall, this is fewer than 5% of all schools in the country. According to Bertha Madras, the White House deputy director of Demand Reduction in the Office of National Drug Policy, the government provided about $1.6 million to public and private schools to conduct drug testing in 2007. Each test costs about $10 to $25, depending on the type of test.

Some states test students for recreational drugs such as marijuana, cocaine, and methamphetamines. Other states, such as New Jersey, test for steroids. In many cases, schools begin testing students for drug use in response to tragic events involving drugs. For example, in 2007, a high school quarterback in Georgia died

THE COST OF DRUGS TO SOCIETY

A study published in 1992 for the National Institute on Drug Abuse and the National Institute on Alcohol Abuse and Alcoholism provided an estimate of the cost of alcohol and drug abuse to society: $245.7 billion. Of that total, $97.7 billion was due directly to the abuse of illegal drugs and alcohol, but not nicotine.

These estimates took into account the costs due to **substance abuse** treatment, healthcare, drug prevention, loss of job earnings, and costs due to crime. This estimate in cost was a 50% increase over the 1985 estimate. The increase is due to four major causes:

- heavy cocaine use
- the rise in cases of **HIV/AIDS**
- more states jailing people for drug-related crimes
- an increase in crimes involving drugs

Drug-related crimes made up about 50% of the $97.7 billion. Some of the other costs are due to the national workforce's loss of productive workers when they are jailed for drug-related crimes, or hurt or killed in a drug-related crime. Other drug-related costs are the expenses of national drug control programs, police and legal services, and property damage.

when he crashed his car. He was under the influence of cocaine at the time of the crash. Partly in response to this incident, Georgia schools now test students for recreational drug use.

Another issue surrounding school drug testing is whether it actually discourages students from using drugs, as supporters of these programs claim. The Office of National Drug Control Policy points to a successful drug-testing program in schools of Alabama's Autauga County.

In the Autauga County program, students volunteer to be tested because passing the test brings rewards. When a student passes the drug test, he or she is given an ID card that allows them to get discounts from area businesses. On the other hand, students who fail the test (for nicotine, cocaine, amphetamines, **opiates**, and marijuana) must give up the ID card if they have one. The school will also notify parents and offer advice about getting the student help. The student will be able to get the ID card back if he or she passes later drug tests. About half of the seventh and eighth graders in the 2001 to 2002 school year participated in this program. Autauga County schools report reductions in drug use among the students: an 11% drop in nicotine use, 9% drop in alcohol use, and about a 7% drop in marijuana use.

Yet, other evidence does not support the usefulness of drug testing in schools. Two independent studies conducted by researchers, who noted their findings in the *Journal of School Health* in 2003, show that school drug testing doesn't reduce drug use by students. This research supports the idea that the best way to predict student drug use is to examine their attitudes toward drug use and examine if their peers use drugs.

WHO IS MOST LIKELY TO SAY "YES" TO DRUGS?

Young people who use drugs do so for various reasons. One reason is to belong to a particular social group. If a person admires members of a certain social group, and the people in that group use drugs, the person might feel pressured to use drugs, too, in order to get into that group. This is one form of peer pressure. Someone under peer pressure might choose to use drugs even if he or she had previously decided not to use them.

Another reason why people might begin to use drugs is because they don't have people in their lives to tell them otherwise. They don't have people in their lives to encourage them to stay away from drugs. A positive role model provides a good example by making choices that are better for his or her health and well-being. A role model can be a family member, including a parent or older sibling. Other role models may include a friend, neighbor, teacher, coach, or community leader.

Someone else might use drugs if he or she is unaware of the consequences of using them. Not everyone knows that illegal drugs are unsafe to use. A trend among illegal drug makers is to make drugs seem less dangerous than they really are. For example, methamphetamine has been combined with strawberry-flavored drink mixes, lollipops, and high-sugar sodas. The "strawberry quick" methamphetamine has been seen in Missouri, Texas, Washington state, and Wisconsin since early 2007. The drugmakers' idea is to remake methamphetamine to look different and taste less bitter. Combining methamphetamine with a sugary substance can mask the strong chemical taste and may make it taste better to first-time users.

One drug in Texas has been gaining popularity since 2005 because of how it has been changed to seem more appealing. Young people are quickly becoming addicted to this drug. The reason for the fast addiction is that the drug—which is called *cheese* because it looks like Parmesan cheese—is a mixture of **heroin** and Tylenol PM powder. Heroin is extremely dangerous and **addictive**, but many young people don't know that cheese contains heroin because it doesn't *look* like heroin. Users are therefore harming themselves more than they know, because they don't really know what they are using and don't know the health consequences of the drug.

SIGNS SOMEONE MIGHT BE USING DRUGS

If you think a friend might be using drugs, ask yourself these questions about his or her recent behavior. If the answer is "yes" to many of these questions, your friend might be using drugs.

- Have they lost interest in school?
- Do they have trouble concentrating in class?
- Do they sleep a lot, even in class?
- Do they get into fights often?
- Do they often have red or puffy eyes?
- Has there been a noticeable weight gain or weight loss, or change in health?
- Do they display extreme changes in mood (negative or worried all the time)?
- Have they changed their friends (to hang out with kids who use drugs)?
- Do they ask to be left alone a lot?

Another reason people use drugs is boredom. Without fun, interesting activities to do in their free time, people might turn to drugs as a way to pass the time instead. A 2003 survey by the National Center on Addiction and Substance Abuse showed that teenagers who describe themselves as "bored" are 50% more likely to smoke, get drunk, and use illegal drugs than teenagers who say they are not often bored. Another factor is stress. Teenagers experiencing a high level of stress are twice as likely to smoke and use drugs compared to teens with low levels of stress. Combining the factors of stress and boredom make a teen more than three times more likely to smoke and use drugs.

2

Drugs in Popular Culture

A person forms his or her opinion about drugs mostly based on the information he or she hears or sees. When you hear or see information about drugs, how do you know whether you're getting someone's opinion or actual facts? Knowing more about who is putting out the information is important, because then you will have an idea about who to trust. Songs, movies, TV, the Internet, and advertising constantly give messages about drugs. Each time drugs are mentioned this way, ask yourself: What are they saying about drugs, and is that message true and safe?

DRUGS IN SONGS

Alcohol and illegal drugs are often mentioned in songs. A 1999 study compiled by the Office of National Drug

Control Policy together with the U.S. Department of Health and Human Services' Substance Abuse and Mental Health Services Administration examined 1,000 popular songs of 1996 and 1997. The study found that 270 of the 1,000 songs mentioned either alcohol or illegal drugs. Of the songs that mentioned illegal drugs, 20% of them linked the drugs with wealth or luxury. Similarly, of the songs that mentioned alcohol, 24% associated alcohol with wealth or luxury. Doing so makes drugs and alcohol seem much more glamorous than they really are.

About 20% of the songs that mentioned drug use brought up the consequences of using illegal drugs. The consequences of alcohol were mentioned in about 9% of the songs that brought up alcohol use. But only 3% of songs that mentioned alcohol contained an anti-alcohol statement. Only 5% of the songs mentioning alcohol contain lyrics describing a refusal of alcohol use. The message of many songs then—and now—is clear: Alcohol and drugs are shown as being acceptable to use, and are even shown as part of a glamorous or exciting way of life.

Not all artists are out there to promote drug and alcohol use. Some, in fact, worry that their songs might be misunderstood. The singer Eric Clapton and his song "Cocaine" are an example. According to an interview with Clapton, he stopped playing the song when he reached out for help for drug addiction and alcoholism. "I thought it might be giving the wrong message to people who were in the same boat as me," he said about his decision to stop playing the song. Later on, however, he changed his mind because the song actually does tell of the realities of drug use. Clapton pointed out, "it very clearly says in the opening verse, 'If you wanna get down, down on the ground.'" He believes that the song talks about the true price of drug use.

A STUDY OF A ROYAL ROLE MODEL

Queen Margrethe II of Denmark, a known chain smoker, was often seen in public with a lit cigarette. But then the Danish monarch began to refrain from smoking in public after antismoking groups and the press criticized her and labeled her the "Ashtray Queen."

Queen Margrethe II of Denmark was the subject of a study published in the scientific journal, *The Lancet*, in 2001. The study examined whether her cigarette smoking was influencing more Danish people to smoke. Queen Margrethe is a popular queen who is known to chain smoke—meaning she smokes cigarettes one right after the other. Her influence on the health of the people of Denmark could be a negative one, researchers believed. The study looked at death rates in Denmark and compared them with other Western countries. Death rates were falling for about five years after Queen Margrethe took the throne, but they rose again after that. Previous studies have already shown that Danish film stars who smoke may influence young women to smoke as well. The Danish government has taken notice: A ban on public smoking in Denmark took effect on April 1, 2007.

DRUGS IN MOVIES

For many years, movies have shown messages about love, friendship, life, and death. They also have passed on ideas about alcohol, **tobacco**, and illegal drugs. A study in 2001, conducted by Kimberly M. Thompson and Fumi Yokota of the Harvard School of Public Health, examined all English language, G-rated, animated feature films released in theaters between 1937 and 2000. Of the 81 films, 47% showed alcohol use and 43% showed tobacco use. Only three of the films gave a message that a character should stop smoking. None of the films contained a message about limiting alcohol. Therefore, the message of almost half of those movies was that alcohol and tobacco use is normal behavior with no long-term consequences.

Exposing young people to images of alcohol and tobacco use raises the concern of what effect it will have on them. Researchers have found some answers to that question. In a 2003 study published in the scientific journal, *The Lancet*, more than 3,000 nonsmoking adolescents were studied to see if watching more movies that showed smoking would increase the number of them who started smoking. The adolescents who had the highest exposure to movies with smoking were 2.7 times more likely to start smoking than were adolescents with less exposure. This is clear evidence that adolescents who view smoking in movies are more likely to start smoking.

This conclusion is especially alarming considering the results of a study published in May 2007 by researchers at Dartmouth Medical School. The study calculated that adolescents in the United States have seen actors smoking on film a total of 13.9 billion times in movies released in theaters between 1998 and 2003. For example, of the 534 movies, the actor Brad Pitt was seen

Although he temporarily gave up smoking to get in shape for his role in the 2004 film *Troy*, actor Brad Pitt's work still sometimes requires him to light up during a movie scene. Outside of work, however, Pitt's life does not reflect the characters he portrays. He has reportedly given up his nicotine habit.

smoking a total of 42 times, and actor Nicholas Cage was seen smoking 37 times.

The influence of movies on adolescents doesn't end with smoking. A study published in the *Journal of Studies on Alcohol* in 2006 came to a similar conclusion regarding movies that show people drinking alcohol. More than 4,000 adolescents were studied to examine a link between their alcohol consumption and their exposure to movies showing alcohol consumption. The conclusion: Teenagers who see alcohol consumption in movies are more likely to start drinking alcohol earlier.

DRUGS ON THE INTERNET

The Internet is a popular source of information about drugs. There are many government and university Web sites that report on information found through scientific research. Also on the Internet are personal Web sites about drugs that express people's personal opinions about drugs.

When viewing Web sites, think about whether you are reading scientific facts or personal opinions. It is important to use good judgment. Think about who created the Web site and what the goal of the site is. Is it a government- or university-sponsored site or a personal Web site? Is the creator of the site trying to sell something? (Some Web sites actually allow the purchase of medications such as Vicodin and OxyContin without a prescription. A study released in 2006 by The National Center on Addiction and Substance Abuse at Columbia University and Beau Dietl & Associates found that 89% of the Web sites researched didn't require a prescription.) Besides actual drugs, is the Web site trying to "sell" a lifestyle that is unhealthy? Is the information trustworthy? Keep these things in mind when reading Web sites that discuss drugs and drug use.

ADVERTISING DRUGS

Advertising takes many forms, from billboards and TV to radio, the Internet, magazine ads, and newspaper ads. Since the purpose of advertising is to sell a product, the ads you see are made to capture your attention and interest. But a problem arises when the item being sold is a legal drug such as tobacco, and its ads catch the attention of young people.

For many years, Camel cigarettes used ads featuring a cartoon camel called "Old Joe" or "Joe Camel." Studies determined that the Joe Camel character was as recognizable as Mickey Mouse to children. The Joe Camel ads were more successful in advertising cigarettes to children than adults: The estimated Camel cigarette sales among young people were estimated to be $470 million per year. In 1997, the U.S. Federal Trade Commission charged the R.J. Reynolds Tobacco Company with breaking laws against the advertisement of addictive substances to people under the age of 18. Two months later, the ads were discontinued.

Advertisers want to sell a product and make money. It may not always be in your best interest to purchase what they are selling. When you see an advertisement, think about how it makes you feel. Does it suggest that you'll be a better person if you use the product? How would the advertiser know it would make you a better person?

DRUGS IN SPORTS

Athletes sometimes use dangerous or illegal substances to improve their performance. This practice is referred to as *doping*. Three common forms of doping include **blood transfusions**, taking **stimulants**, and taking **narcotics**. The performance-enhancing effects and side effects of doping vary, depending on what is used.

For 23 years, the tobacco company R.J. Reynolds used Joe Camel to promote cigarette consumption in young people. One study showed that 90% of children were able to associate the image of Joe Camel with a cigarette, while only 67% of adults could recognize the cartoon character.

An athlete can receive a blood transfusion that contains extra hemoglobin molecules. Hemoglobin molecules carry oxygen in your blood. Therefore, more

DRUGS AND PRO WRESTLING

In 2006, after the deaths of some of its top wrestlers, the organization World Wrestling Entertainment (WWE) started randomly testing for illegal drugs, steroids, and prescription drugs. The death of wrestler Eddie Guerrero in 2005 might have been what made the organization start drug testing, but many other wrestlers had died before him. Since 1997, about 65 of a total of 1,000 wrestlers have died. Of the 65 wrestlers, 25 died from heart attacks or other heart problems. The controversy surrounding the WWE is that the culture of wrestling is built upon the use of steroids and other drugs to build the large-muscled bodies of its wrestlers. Popular former wrestlers including Jesse Ventura, who went on to serve as the governor of Minnesota, have admitted to using steroids.

Because of steroid and drug use, wrestlers "have death rates about seven times higher than the general U.S. population," explained Keith Pinckard, a Dallas medical examiner. He added, "They are 12 times more likely to die from heart disease than other Americans 25 to 44." A common **side effect** of using steroids is an enlarged or weakened heart. But with the top wrestlers earning more than $1 million per year, many aspiring wrestlers put their health at risk in the hopes of becoming rich and famous.

WWE's random drug testing policy started in February 2006 and is called the Talent Wellness Program. It bans

oxygen can be delivered to an athlete's muscles while he or she is competing. This can increase his or her endurance, which can be especially helpful in long distance

WWE wrestler Chris Benoit *(left)* died in a murder-suicide, in which he allegedly killed his wife and son before hanging himself. His autopsy revealed that he had steroids in his system at the time of his death, which could have triggered an uncontrollable spell of violent anger, commonly known as "'roid rage."

the use of **performance-enhancing drugs** that are taken for reasons other than a real medical purpose. Drugs received over the Internet with a prescription are not allowed. In August of 2007, 10 wrestlers were suspended under the Talent Wellness Program for using steroids and other banned drugs. The names of the suspended wrestlers were kept secret, but the names of future offenders will be made public.

events like cycling. In the case of blood transfusions, the side effects include kidney damage, diseases caught from dirty needles, and problems with blood flow. Stimulants are another performance enhancer. They are used to make a person more alert and to help him or her fight fatigue. One side effect of taking stimulants is increased hostility. Cocaine and caffeine are two banned stimulants in sports. Athletes might also use narcotics as painkillers. Narcotics allow an athlete to tolerate a higher level of pain. But the downside is that he or she may wind up with worse injuries due to not being aware of an injury soon enough to treat it. Addiction and **physical dependence** could result from the use of stimulants and narcotics.

Anabolic steroids are another common doping substance. They are used to grow muscle at an extremely fast rate that is not normal for healthy people. Steroid abuse can lead to higher risks for heart attack, **stroke**, and liver problems. Other effects can include the shrinking of genital organs and breast development in men. These effects are more serious for adolescents since their bodies are still growing.

The problem of steroid use among athletes has caused many people to become alarmed enough to do something about it. In 2003, the insurance company Blue Cross/Blue Shield released results of a study showing that about 1.1 million teens have used some form of performance-enhancing drug or supplement. In his 2004 State of the Union address, President George W. Bush drew attention to the problem. He said that athletics were important to the American people but "some in professional sports are not setting much of an example." Bush continued by saying that the "use of performance-enhancing drugs like steroids in baseball, football, and other sports is dangerous, and it sends the wrong message." He called on "team owners, union represen-tatives, coaches, and players to take the lead, to send the right signal, to get tough, and to get rid of steroids now."

From cycling to baseball, stories of drug use in sports seem to be getting more and more common in the news. Performance-enhancing drugs have been linked with some of the biggest names in sports. The 2006 Tour de France winner, Floyd Landis, is still arguing the decision to disqualify him after he tested positive for banned **testosterone** supplements. In 2007, four rid-ers were dropped from the race due to testing positive for banned performance-enhancing substances. Baseball player Mark McGwire has admitted to using androstene-dione, which is similar to an anabolic steroid. When the U.S. Congress held a hearing in 2005 to investigate the use of drugs in sports, McGwire was asked about other drugs he had used. He would not say.

Sometimes athletes' involvement with drugs has deadly consequences. One example is baseball player Ken Caminiti, who was named Most Valuable Player in 1996 for the National League. In 2002, he admitted to using steroids during 1996 and abusing alcohol and painkillers early in his career. He retired from baseball in 2001, but not from drug use. On October 10, 2004, Caminiti was found dead at 41 years old from an **over-dose** of cocaine and opiates. It was ruled that his death was due to the weakening of his heart from drugs.

A more recent case also involved a baseball player who used cocaine extensively. Rodney Beck was a three-time All Star relief pitcher in the National League. According to his ex-wife, he "had a disease of addiction, which is a brain disease, and it stole him away from the people he loved." Beck was found dead at his house on June 23, 2007. He was 38 years old and had battled his addiction for three

In 2005, former St. Louis Cardinals slugger Mark McGwire *(above)* participated in a Congressional hearing concerning the use of steroids in baseball. Although he was accused by former teammate Jose Canseco of using steroids to further his career, McGwire would not answer questions on past drug abuse. Members of Congress in attendance at the hearing criticized baseball officials for not policing its athletes, while allowing, and perhaps even encouraging, the use of performance-enhancing drugs in the game.

years. Two attempts at drug treatment and an intervention by his family three weeks before his death weren't able to save him.

3

Where to Learn About Drugs

To get the real facts about drugs, people need to get information from sources they can trust—from people or organizations that have their best interests in mind. For preteens and teens, these people might include parents, teachers, and other adults at school who want them to be healthy and safe. Also, there are many organizations that provide current and accurate information about scientific research on drugs.

FIRST STEP: TALK TO YOUR PARENTS

It might sound weird or uncomfortable to talk to your parents about drugs, but you may be glad you did. By talking with them, you will be starting a conversation about an important subject. You will also be creating

"MY X-TREME LIFE," BY TAUNY VENTURA

Everyone told me that I should try it—that I would love it and it would give me such a rush. I was scared, but I am curious by nature and I knew I would probably love it once I got my feet wet. So I did it: I swam with sharks! It was one of the most exciting and thrilling experiences of my life.

These are the types of healthy risks I take in my life—the kind that give me an incomparable adrenaline rush. By trying new things and living my life to the fullest, I've made the decision that drinking and drugs are unnecessary in my world.

I'm grateful that both my parents were open and honest with me whenever I asked questions [about drugs]. They doled out lots of factual information regarding health issues and drugs, which I found really helpful. Their love, guidance, attention, and support squashed any desires I might have had to drink or try drugs.

I was very involved in high school extra-curricular activities. I joined clubs as well as varsity track and I also participated in school musicals. My typical high-school day often started at 7 A.M. and went until midnight. I didn't have time for drugs because I was too involved and, plus, it just wasn't me.

College has been a whole new experience; I was away from home and I didn't have Mom or Dad looking over my shoulder. I became involved in other activities at school—the more active I am, the happier I am. I went

out for Class Senate, and also landed a role as one of the main dancers in a modern-day production of Julius Caesar.

I found time to make new friends and we often attended campus parties. I never really cared for drinking beer and when I was offered a can by my friends, I easily said no while they looked at me as if I had three heads. They soon realized that I could still be the life of a party without drinking or doing drugs.

I've now made it through my junior year and I've also faced many more situations involving drugs and alcohol. And I've consistently stayed away. I can honestly say that I am proud of who I am and the choices I've made—I won't let drugs define me.

I try to fill my life with activities that give me excitement in ways drugs never could. I love snowboarding, whitewater rafting, and am soon going skydiving with the X-treme sports club.

When I spend time with my family, friends, and boyfriend and dare myself to take healthy risks, it's the most **euphoric***, unexplainable, unique feeling that I doubt any artificial high could surpass. I do what I do, I am who I am, and I simply refuse to let drugs get in the way of being the best I can be.*

Source: Reprinted with permission from Checkyourself.com, 2007.

trust and open communication that can help when dealing with other difficult issues. You might know what your parents' stand is about drug use, but you may not know their reasoning behind it. It's important to hear what they have to say, and to ask them questions. They may know a lot more than you think, and you know you can trust what they are telling you.

TALK TO YOUR TEACHERS

Many people have at least one teacher with whom they connect and can trust. That teacher is a good person to approach when having questions about drugs. What better place than a school to gain information about a topic? A science or health teacher in particular

THE STRAIGHTWAY TEAM

The StraightWay Team is a group of young performers who use their talents to spread the message of making good life choices. They use original music, drama, and comedy, as well as dance and motivational speaking during their concert-style assemblies. The group was founded 20 years ago in Texas and performed mostly within the state early on. Now, however, the team is branching out to other cities and states, as well as Europe.

The team consists of 8 to 10 young people who actually follow the message that they teach. They use personal stories about overcoming obstacles in their lives and seeking out positive things, rather than the negative. They reach about 700,000 students each year in about 1,500

would be able to explain, in detail, a drug's effect on the body.

Also, some schools have begun programs that address issues of drug use. Many schools are conducting school-wide discussions about drugs and alcohol in an effort to inform students. There are many opportunities at your school to find answers to questions about drugs, because teachers and school staff want to help their students make informed decisions.

DRUG PREVENTION AND RESOURCES

There are many organizations aiming to help young people learn about and stay away from drugs. What follows is a summary of some of these organizations.

presentations. As a way to continue working towards the goal of helping young people, 70 StraightWay Clubs have been started in Texas schools. The clubs provide extra training and back-up for the StraightWay vision for young people.

The StraightWay Web site has more information about drugs and other issues affecting teens. Through the site, you can also purchase CDs of the original music written and recorded by the members of the StraightWay Team. As governor of Texas, George W. Bush applauded the StraightWay group for its "efforts to promote drug prevention and treatment in Texas public schools. [In doing your work,] you help improve [young people's] chances for success in life."

D.A.R.E.

D.A.R.E. stands for Drug Abuse Resistance Education. It serves millions of students in the United States and around the world. The program operates in 75% of school districts in the United States, reaching kindergarteners to twelfth graders, to bring the message of how to live a life without drugs, violence, and gangs. Police officers conduct the lessons and coach students through activities such as resisting peer pressure. Officers go through special training before taking on the job of D.A.R.E. educator.

The program was created in 1983 in Los Angeles, California. Its curriculum has been changed over the years to include information based on the latest research and to meet the changing needs of its students. In 2006, for example, a newly created middle school program used mock court trials to help students understand the legal consequences of drug use.

Besides giving out important information about drugs, D.A.R.E. also provides creative extra-curricular activities for students. One of these is the D.A.R.E. Dance program, an after-school program in middle schools. After seeing a professional dance group perform at an assembly, students are invited to participate in a free 10-week dance class. The high point of the class is a dance performance by participating students. If students are committed to continuing their dance instruction, they can apply for scholarships at local dance studios. More information about D.A.R.E., as well as information about drugs, can be found at its Web site, www.dare.com.

YOUTH TO YOUTH INTERNATIONAL

Youth to Youth is an award-winning drug prevention program that focuses on encouraging middle and high school students to live without using tobacco, alcohol, and other drugs. This group was founded in 1982 in Columbus, Ohio. It hosts conferences that aim to help

A COMMUNITY LEADER AGAINST METHAMPHETAMINES

Susan York has seen what drug addiction can do to a person. Her mother lost her battle with addiction and died of an overdose while Susan was in high school. So when York suspected that her neighbor's house was being used as a laboratory to make a drug called crystal methamphetamine, she knew she had to do something about it.

Susan York kept track of the ongoing parties and drug use and called the police. While the police made 25 arrests at the house over two years, they didn't have the power to permanently shut down the house. Frustrated, Susan and another area neighbor, Travis Talbot, started Lead on America, which stands for Law Enforcement Against Drugs in Our Neighborhoods, in 2001. The mission of the group is to give people the tools and information needed to combat a meth house in their neighborhood.

The group works very closely with local law enforcement and shares information with neighbors. It also shows neighbors how to properly report information to the police and get other government agencies involved in an effort to shut down a meth house. For instance, neighbors can report trash or rodent problems to the health department. They can also alert local counselors and police if there is a child being neglected by a meth-addicted parent. If the home is run-down and there are abandoned cars surrounding it, they can call the proper authorities to handle that. It takes multiple organizations and violations to finally shut down a meth lab.

So far, Lead on America has played a part in shutting down 38 suspected meth houses. Susan York has worked

(continues on page 44)

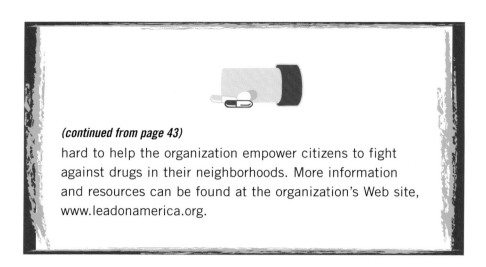

(continued from page 43)
hard to help the organization empower citizens to fight against drugs in their neighborhoods. More information and resources can be found at the organization's Web site, www.leadonamerica.org.

young people build problem-solving skills and deal with issues surrounding peer pressure to use drugs.

This program is unique in that teenagers make up a large portion of the staff that conducts the trainings and workshops. Young people help plan and coordinate special events as well. Professional speakers are also used to strengthen the message and get it across to a wide audience. Hundreds of communities across the United States have used the Youth to Youth example to construct similar drug use prevention programs. More than 300,000 people across the country have been in touch with the programs of Youth to Youth International. More information about Youth to Youth International and their events can be found at their Web site at www.y2yint.com.

SADD

SADD (Students Against Destructive Decisions) was originally founded in 1981 as Students Against Drunk Driving. It has since expanded its message to include other issues, such as negative peer pressure, substance abuse, violence, and suicide. The mission of SADD is to provide young people with the tools to deal with those issues.

In order to help young people stay informed about the issues they face daily, Students Against Destructive Decisions (SADD) organizes local events for students and community members to learn about teen issues, such as peer pressure and substance abuse. Here, a student participates in an activity involving "drunk goggles," which are glasses that simulate how a person's vision is distorted while under the influence of alcohol.

Like Youth to Youth International, SADD uses young people to conduct peer-to-peer workshops, trainings, forums, and conferences throughout the organization's thousands of chapters in middle schools, high schools, and colleges. SADD has been active in many ways to reduce drug use among young people. It has launched its own programs and given its support to other existing programs.

Getting the message out about issues that affect young people is one of the strengths of SADD. It is able to accomplish that through its 350,000 active members in 10,000 chapters located in schools and colleges. To get more information about SADD, check out its Web site at www.sadd.org.

NIDA FOR TEENS

The National Institute on Drug Abuse is a branch of the National Institutes of Health, which is one of the most respected science and health organizations in the world. NIDA for Teens is a Web site that provides a vast amount of helpful information about drugs and their effects. The site includes, among other things, self-quizzes about drug use and information about how the brain is affected by specific drugs. There is also a useful glossary to look up drug-related words you may not know, and links to other related Web sites, including one about club drugs. NIDA's Web site for teens can be found at http://teens.drugabuse.gov.

4

Commonly Abused Legal Drugs

Just because a drug is legally available doesn't mean it can't harm people. Someone can abuse a legal drug by using it in excessive amounts (alcohol, for example) or by using it for an unintended purpose (such as strong medications). What follows is information about some of the most commonly abused legal drugs.

ALCOHOL ABUSE

In 2003, 23% of people who went to public drug treatment centers went there for alcohol abuse. Drinks like beer, wine, and liquor contain a kind of alcohol called **ethanol**, which is responsible for the drink's effect on the body. One 12-ounce beer, one 5-ounce glass of wine, and one 1.5-ounce shot of liquor all contain the same amount of ethanol.

Many people drink alcohol because they say it makes them feel relaxed. A reason for this response is the way alcohol works in the body. Alcohol slows the activity of the brain and nerves, which leads to poor coordination and reflexes. When under the influence of alcohol, a person may not be able to walk in a straight line and cannot drive a car safely. Another effect of being under the influence is that a person's inhibitions—feelings that stop people from acting on every thought they have—are lowered. Inhibitions are what keep people from making decisions without thinking, such as starting a fight with another person, or doing something sexual with someone before they are ready. While under the influence of alcohol, people may not be able to make good decisions to keep themselves safe.

Other symptoms of alcohol abuse can include slurred speech, breathing difficulties, blackouts, and coma, which result from higher doses. The act of binge drinking can cause these serious symptoms to arise. Binge drinking is defined as drinking five or more drinks in one session for a male, and four or more drinks for a female.

Drinking this heavily can have serious long-term consequences. With heavy drinking comes an increased chance of dependence on alcohol. And when a person starts drinking earlier in life, he or she also increases his or her chances of falling into the trap of alcoholism. Even more, scientific research shows that a person's brain may not be fully developed by 20 years of age, and may not develop to its maximum potential if he or she consumes alcohol regularly before age 21. Excessive drinking over a long period of time can cause permanent damage to many other parts of the body, including the liver and the brain. Besides damaging brain cells, the body responds to alcohol by "adapting" to operate with alcohol present. This means that in order to get the same

Many people believe that wine and beer contains less alcohol than hard liquor. As this image portrays, however, the alcohol in one shot of liquor is equal to the amount in a glass of wine or a pint of beer.

"pleasant feelings" next time, a person may have to consume more alcohol. This increase makes drinking even more dangerous.

NICOTINE ABUSE

Nicotine is a drug found naturally in tobacco leaves. Tobacco leaves are processed to make cigarettes of many different types; it can also be chewed, or even sniffed.

Tobacco that is not smoked—called smokeless tobacco—is sometimes referred to as chew, dip, spit tobacco, or snuff.

When a cigarette is smoked, nicotine is absorbed into the bloodstream after only eight seconds. Once in the blood, nicotine acts like a messenger of the brain. It causes the heart and lungs to work faster, and releases sugars into the bloodstream. These actions are part of the reason a person might feel stimulated, or more energetic, after smoking a cigarette.

Another reason a smoker feels stimulated is the other effect of nicotine: It causes the release of large amounts of a natural chemical known as dopamine. Dopamine is responsible for causing feelings of pleasure in the brain. It is usually released in association with feelings such as love, or during comforting moments. After using nicotine, pleasurable feelings will then be linked with smoking a cigarette or chewing smokeless tobacco. The actions of nicotine in the brain last about 40 minutes, which is why users must smoke or chew more tobacco soon after they smoke or chew to continue feeling its stimulating effects. These actions lead to frequent use of nicotine.

Because nicotine causes such large amounts of dopamine to be released, the brain makes adjustments in how dopamine is released normally. The brain will reduce the amount it releases without nicotine present, and also reduces the number of places in the brain where dopamine can perform its actions. Therefore, a person who uses a lot of tobacco will have to begin using it just to bring his or her dopamine levels up to normal. This means the person will feel irritable and unhappy unless

Many people who use smokeless tobacco (also known as chewing tobacco) believe it is a safe alternative to smoking cigarettes. Studies have shown, however, that chewing tobacco contains three to four times the amount of addictive nicotine found in cigarettes and can lead to oral cancer and lesions.

he or she smokes or chews tobacco to get nicotine's effect. This is what causes the craving for tobacco, and what makes nicotine extremely addictive. Heroin and cocaine cause similar changes in the brain.

What makes matters more difficult for someone who is already addicted is that cigarettes today contain more nicotine than in the past. Heavy smoking also causes lung cancer and other lung diseases that contribute to 500,000 deaths in the United States each year. Teens who smoke also are more likely to have panic attacks—problems with intense fear and nerves that come up for seemingly no reason—and depression compared to non-smoking teens.

THE ABUSE OF INHALANTS

Inhalants are chemicals that are sniffed through the nose and/or mouth to cause an effect on the mind. Many are found in household products, which make them accessible to young people. Common slang names for inhalants include laughing gas, snappers, poppers, whippets, bold, and rush. Inhalants fall into three categories based on the type of chemical: solvents, gases, and nitrites. Solvents include paint thinner, correction fluid, gasoline, and glue. Gases include those found in whipped cream dispensers, butane lighters, spray paint, and nitrous oxide. Nitrites are found in room deodorizers and perfumes.

Inhalants are taken in through the mouth or nose in different ways. Sniffing, snorting, or huffing refers to taking in the fumes of certain inhalants. Chemicals in a kind of can called an aerosol can are sprayed into the nose or mouth. Once the chemicals are taken into the lungs, they are quickly carried around the body in the bloodstream. Users feel a high that only lasts a few minutes. Other effects of inhalant use are hallucinations, dizziness, poor coordination, slurred speech, and headaches. The symptoms increase and gradually worsen the more they are used.

Many times, more than one chemical is entering the body when someone uses an inhalant. Some chemicals leave the body quickly, while others linger, causing continued or even permanent effects on the body. Some chemicals are stored in the fatty parts of brain cells. Damage to these cells will hurt their ability to control basic functions in the body, such as walking and talking. A person's limbs may tremble as a result of the damage. The cells in the brain where memory is controlled can also be impaired. A person might therefore have

"ADDICTED TO INHALANTS," BY MEGAN HAKEMAN

I never thought it could happen to me. Becoming addicted to inhalants was not a plan that I had. I had a pretty good childhood, playing sports and hanging out with my brother and neighborhood friends. My mom and I were close, and we would spend quite a bit of time together.

But I had many problems. Although a lot of teens probably feel as though they have problems, mine were rooted in something that wasn't my fault: sexual abuse. Dealing with something such as this, alone, is virtually an impossible task, and at the time, it felt impossible to overcome. Therefore, I needed to cope. Life was becoming too much for me, and when I was offered help to begin a healing process, I refused it. I felt nothing at that time would help, until I encountered drugs.

It really seemed as though getting high was helping me forget my problems. That's when I began huffing—you know, inhaling various household products to get high. I inhaled almost anything I could get my hands on— computer cleaner, air freshener, various spray bottles, etc.—so that I could get high.

My parents knew something wasn't right, and they would drag me to counseling. I learned, though, that when one starts inhaling, she can be very sneaky so that she doesn't lose an opportunity to get high. I did it alone, I did it with friends, I did it when I felt sad, lonely, or scared— even when I was happy. It was my escape—I didn't care about family, friends, life, or anything.

(continues on page 54)

(continued from page 53)

In treatment I learned how to communicate my feelings instead of hiding from them through drugs. Even though I hated treatment for the first month, it was the best thing that could have happened, because I changed in so many ways. Now I am able to talk about my thoughts and feelings, instead of covering them up. I was in treatment for three months, and actually, I feel lucky. In fact, I know I am lucky. Huffing could have killed me. I started to huff when I was 13 years old . . . that's too young to do a lot of things, including becoming an addict, or dying.

I recently celebrated my fifteenth birthday as a sober, healthy, high school student, and to be honest, staying sober can be challenging at times. Kids in school definitely huff to get high, and some even ask me to participate even though they know what I've been through. Trust me, I have no plans to ever get high again. I never want to go through that nightmare again. An important lesson I learned when I got out of treatment was that my supposed friends who I used to get high with only liked me when I was high. I also realized that I didn't like me when I was high.

Source: Reprinted with permission
from Checkyourself.com, 2007.

difficulty learning new things, or even carrying on a conversation.

Long-term use of inhalants can also cause serious damage to important organs in the body. Besides damage to the brain, liver failure can occur, and permanent damage to the heart can result as well. Through the continued use of butane, propane, and chemicals in aerosols, the heart's natural beating rhythm can be interrupted, causing death.

ANABOLIC STEROID ABUSE

Anabolic steroids are a kind of human-made drug similar to testosterone, a male sex hormone. Doctors prescribe anabolic steroids to help patients who make too little testosterone or have other health problems. Recreational use of anabolic steroids, often called *roids* or *juice*, is illegal. The term *anabolic* refers to the building of muscle. People will abuse them in order to increase the amount of muscle on their bodies. Anabolic steroids can be taken in pill form or injected directly into muscle.

Even though using anabolic steroids will build large amounts of muscle fast, there are severe consequences for the user. Liver cancer, high blood pressure, kidney tumors, and severe acne are just some of the physical effects of using steroids. Because of the fact that anabolic steroids are similar to testosterone, they will mix up the male and female sexual characteristics of users. The testicles of males may shrink. Also, males may have a lower sperm count, baldness, and develop breasts. Women may grow facial hair, become bald, experience a change in menstrual cycle, and develop a deeper voice. Adolescents, who haven't finished growing yet, may permanently stunt their growth by using steroids.

Other effects of using anabolic steroids involve behavior changes. Users may experience extreme mood swings and aggression. These mood swings can lead to violent behavior. Other feelings that can arise are extreme anger, delusions, and the feeling that one can do anything and can't be beaten. Of steroid abusers who seek treatment, about 10% say they moved on to other drugs as a way to deal with some of the side effects of anabolic steroid use. It is therefore possible that anabolic steroid use could lead to other drug use.

PRESCRIPTION DRUG ABUSE: OXYCONTIN

Many medical drugs need a permission note from a doctor, called a prescription. This is to keep people from using strong medical drugs for nonmedical purposes. But in 1999, about 9 million Americans did just that: used prescription medications to get high. For example, painkillers such as OxyContin are crushed and snorted. This makes the drug act faster and results in a stronger effect than it normally has when taken as instructed. This improper use of OxyContin has increased by 40% over the last three years among high school students in the twelfth grade. As of 2005, 5.5% of high school twelfth graders reported using OxyContin as a recreational drug.

Using prescription drugs inappropriately might seem like a safer alternative to using drugs such as cocaine, because prescription drugs are made legally by a company. The problem, however, is that prescription drugs are only intended to be used as directed by the doctor. Also, a user might not be aware of how easy it is to become addicted to these drugs.

Furthermore, when they become addicted, users will often resort to theft or using fake prescriptions to continue using OxyContin. OxyContin normally costs about four dollars for a 40-milligram pill when purchased for a real medical issue. On the street, it can sell for ten times that price. People addicted to OxyContin will sometimes even switch to heroin because it is the cheaper of the two drugs.

Families protest outside a Virginia courtroom where three executives of Purdue Pharma were on trial for misbranding OxyContin to the public. The company's aggressive efforts to market the drug as a safe and effective painkiller misled doctors and patients, resulting in widespread addiction and fatal overdoses. The executives pled guilty and were ordered to serve four years of probation and pay $634 million in fines.

OxyContin belongs to a group of drugs called **opioids**, which are drugs that are used to relieve pain. Two other commonly abused prescription drugs that are opioids are Vicodin and Demerol. When combined with other drugs such as alcohol or allergy medicines, opioids can have life-threatening effects.

Physical dependence can occur if a person abuses opioids for a long period of time, because the body has adjusted to the drug always being there. The brain also becomes adjusted to having the drug present. This can happen even when using the drug as prescribed by a doctor. A doctor will instruct his or her patient to gradually use less and less of the drug—a process known as "stepping-down"—until he or she reaches a point where he or she can stop using it entirely. If a person all of a sudden stops taking a drug after using it for a long period of time, he or she will experience **withdrawal**. Withdrawal symptoms can include vomiting, cold flashes, diarrhea, insomnia, restlessness, muscle pain, and bone pain.

Physical dependence is not the same thing as addiction, though. Addiction is an uncontrollable craving for a substance that leads to destructive behaviors in order to obtain that substance. Someone can have a physical dependence on something, but not necessarily be addicted to it. However, in addition to physical dependence, addiction is likely to occur if these prescription drugs are used improperly.

5

Illegal Drugs That Are Abused

Illegal drugs are never safe to use. Laws have been passed against many kinds of drugs in an attempt to protect people from using them and harming themselves. Abuse of many of these drugs can lead to physical dependence and addiction.

MARIJUANA ABUSE

Marijuana is the most commonly abused illegal drug in the United States. But just because it is common, that does not mean that *everyone* is using it. In fact, as stated in Chapter 1, marijuana use among eighth, tenth, and twelfth graders has decreased each year since 1997. Only about 1 in 6 tenth graders is currently using marijuana. Also, fewer than 1 in 4 twelfth graders is currently using marijuana.

Marijuana goes by more than 200 different street names, including pot, weed, herb, and chronic, just to name a few. Stronger forms of marijuana go by the names hashish (or hash) and sinsemilla. Users smoke or ingest the dried parts of the hemp plant. Smoking marijuana usually involves wrapping the dried marijuana in cigarette or cigar wrappers. Marijuana can also be mixed with food and eaten.

The chemical responsible for marijuana's brain-changing effect is delta-9-tetrahydrocannabinol, or THC for short. Marijuana's effects vary depending on how much THC it contains, the user's previous experience with marijuana, and whether other drugs are used along with it. The effects of marijuana usually start within 10 minutes of using it and last for 3 to 4 hours. Someone using marijuana might feel relaxed and sleepy and have a short attention span. It also alters how the person sees his or her environment and can make it feel as though time passes very slowly. Users sometimes also feel paranoid and anxious.

THC causes communication problems in the brain in order to make these effects happen. It also causes a drop in blood pressure and a loss in coordination, and affects how memory works. The areas of the brain that are affected are known as the hippocampus, the cerebellum, and the basal ganglion. The hippocampus is where learning and memory are controlled. A person using marijuana might have trouble learning new things or remembering recent events. The cerebellum is responsible for balance and coordination. A person using marijuana might be less able to perform in sports or other physically demanding activities. The basal ganglion is the part of the brain involved in controlling body movement. Someone using marijuana would have difficulty driving a car because he or she would not be able to

Despite its negative health effects, marijuana remains one of the most commonly abused drugs in the United States. While some people believe it has medicinal properties, studies have shown marijuana abuse can lead to lung cancer and other problems relating to everyday activities that involve concentration, including driving.

react as quickly to conditions on the road, such as stop signs or other cars.

Besides affecting the brain, marijuana also affects the heart and lungs. After the first hour of smoking marijuana, the user's risk of a heart attack increases by more than four times. Frequent smokers of marijuana have more health problems than nonsmokers. These health problems have to do mostly with the lungs. Smoking marijuana can double or triple the risk of developing certain types of cancer, especially lung cancer. Marijuana smoke contains as much tar as tobacco smoke and 50% to 70% more carcinogenic hydrocarbons (a particular type of chemical) than tobacco smoke. Marijuana smokers tend to hold the smoke in their lungs longer than tobacco smokers, which also exposes their lungs to more cancer-causing chemicals.

"HI, MY NAME IS DAVE AND I WAS A POTHEAD," BY DAVE

I had a pretty normal childhood. I was never too outwardly social. I was a little shy. I smoked pot for the first time the summer after my sophomore year of high school. I had made up my mind that I wanted to try it.

I started using a couple times a month. I was in a youth group—and about half of us got high one night together. We got caught and were kicked out of the group. My mother made me see a therapist, but I didn't think I needed to be there. My parents told me that if they caught me again, they were going to send me to rehab. I stopped smoking after that until the summer before college.

I started college at Columbia University. On the first day, I got high with a new friend on my floor. I got high every day that week. Then I used on a daily basis. When the spring semester came I started to deal drugs. I started to do worse and worse in school. I was starting to become reckless as well. I used to drive high all the time.

During summer break, I was pretty much smoking daily when I was home and around my family. They knew I was using and dealing and they made arrangements for me to go to rehab. I was angry with my parents and didn't think I had a problem. My parents said, "Either you go to rehab or you find another place to live and another way to pay your

Also, THC blocks the immune system from fighting diseases, so if a person develops a disease, his or her body is less able to fight it.

college tuition." I knew school was important and I didn't want to live on the street.

June 4, 2005, was my first day clean.

I had decided that I would go to treatment with an open mind. They had a guest speaker come in—a kid who had been there the year before me. I realized that this kid's story was just like mine, but he kept using and his life spiraled out of control. He wound up alone, hopeless, and depressed, with no place to go. I thought, "I don't want that for my life. I want a future." I decided I would listen more, look at the readings more.

I'm a junior at Columbia studying civil engineering. Over the summer, I worked at an engineering company and lived at home with my family. I spend a bunch of time with my friends from the meetings at Road Recovery. I have more clarity and better and more reliable friends now than I ever had when I was using drugs.

If you think you have a problem, ask yourself this: "Does my use of drugs cause negative consequences in my life?" If the answer is yes, you may have a problem. At least keep an open mind—ask for help and try to find resources.

Source: Reprinted with permission from Checkyourself.com, 2007.
Last name omitted by author.

High doses of marijuana can cause hallucinations, impaired memory, and disorientation, too. And contrary to what many people say, marijuana does have the potential to be addictive. It is not physically addictive—meaning that the human body does not adapt to having THC present—but the behavior of smoking itself is extremely addictive. This is known as psychological addiction.

COCAINE AND CRACK ABUSE

Cocaine is a highly addictive drug made from the coca plant. It is processed from the plant into a white powder that can be snorted, rubbed on a person's gums, or injected after being dissolved in water. Some common street names for cocaine are coke, snow, blow, and rock. Crack is a crystal form of cocaine that is smoked.

The snorting of cocaine causes a high that lasts from 15 to 30 minutes. Smoking crack delivers the drug faster to the body and results in a shorter, more intense high, which lasts about 5 to 10 minutes. Cocaine overstimulates the brain and nerves, building up an extreme amount of dopamine. This results in intense feelings of power and euphoria. It also results in the tightening of blood vessels and increases body temperature, heartbeat speed, and blood pressure. The heart must work harder to circulate blood through the body because blood vessels are constricted.

All of this puts a great deal of stress on the body. These changes in the body can lead to health problems including heart attacks, chest pain, inability to breathe, strokes, and seizures. Cocaine also can decrease a person's appetite, which can lead to the user not eating enough important nutrients.

Users of cocaine describe feelings of irritability, anxiety, and intense fear. Some users increase their doses of the drug as an attempt to get the same high that they felt the first time they used the drug. This is extremely dangerous because longtime cocaine users can become sensitive to the drug after repeated use. Therefore, due to this sensitivity, even low doses of cocaine can cause fatal reactions.

Repeated snorting of cocaine can also lead to a loss of smell, nosebleeds, a constantly runny nose, and problems with swallowing. Those who inject cocaine can have severe allergic reactions and are at a greater risk for getting HIV/AIDS and other diseases carried in blood. The use of cocaine, as in other drugs, reduces inhibitions, which makes risky behavior—such as sharing needles or having unprotected sex, which increases the chances of getting HIV—more likely.

Combining two drugs at the same time further increases the risk of harm to the user. Cocaine or crack is sometimes combined with heroin, a combination called a speedball. These drugs may react to each other in a particularly dangerous way, not to mention the individual effects of each drug on the body. Mixing cocaine and alcohol is another hazardous recipe. When cocaine and alcohol are taken together, the liver attempts to process them by combining them to make a substance called cocaethylene. This chemical makes cocaine's euphoric effects more intense, but also makes it more likely that sudden death will occur.

HEROIN ABUSE

Heroin is a drug that is processed from morphine. Morphine is found naturally in the opium poppy plant. Morphine, heroin, and codeine are in a group of pain-relieving drugs called opiates. Doctors prescribe morphine and codeine to patients with mild to severe pain. Heroin, usually found as a white or brown powder, is not used medically. Some common street names for heroin are crank, horse, jive, smack, H, junk, or skag.

The body naturally makes its own opiates, called endorphins. Endorphins are chemical messengers that act to reduce pain in the body. Heroin overstimulates the parts of the brain that normally react to endorphins. This results in a feeling of euphoria at first, as well as warm flushing of the skin and legs and arms that feel heavy. After this, the user becomes sleepy and breathes more slowly. The person's anxiety lessens and his or her thoughts become dull and unclear. Other symptoms of short-term use include stomach upset and cold.

Long-term users will develop a tolerance to the drug, and will increase the dose to get the same high. Increasing the dose increases the chance of physical dependence and addiction. Sudden death by overdosing becomes more likely with increased doses, too. Also, drug dealers might mix heroin and other street drugs with household substances to make them less expensive to produce. For example, heroin is sometimes mixed with laundry detergents and cleaners or rat poison. These substances can cause clogs in the blood vessels that go to major organs. This leads to the death of cells in those organs. Other problems for long-term users include collapsed veins, heart infections, liver disease, and skin infections.

MDMA ABUSE

MDMA is short for methylenedioxymethamphetamine. It's much easier to refer to it by the name most people call it: **Ecstasy**. Other common names include E, XTC, Adam, hug, beans, clarity, and love drug. Ecstasy is a drug that people make in drug labs, many times in their own homes.

Ecstasy makes its user feel more alert and energetic. It is often used at dance clubs and parties because it

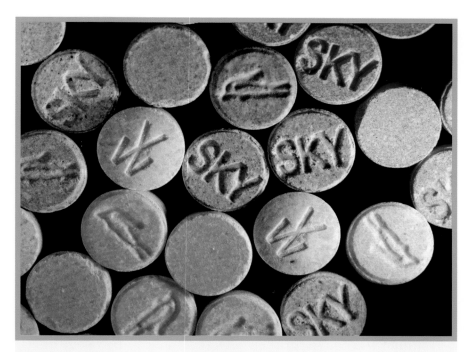

Normally used at clubs and parties, Ecstasy's danger not only lies in its possible toxic affects on the brain, but also in its composition. Often mixed in drug labs in people's homes, these pills sometimes contain other drug substances, such as cocaine, PCP, or methamphetamine, all of which can result in adverse reactions in the human body.

allows the user to dance for hours and hours. A **hit** of MDMA lasts for 3 to 6 hours. The peak of the hit for the user is after about 45 minutes, and then the drug's effects begin to decrease in intensity. Ecstasy also causes the user to hallucinate, experience a stronger sense of touch, and to see the world differently. The user may also have sweating, chills, dizziness, and blurred vision.

MDMA users can become dehydrated as a result of dancing and sweating for such a long time. This can lead to an increase in body temperature, called hyperthermia.

Hyperthermia is dangerous because it can lead to kidney, liver, and heart problems, and sometimes even death. This can occur especially when a person takes "bumps," or multiple doses in a short time.

The side effects of Ecstasy include feelings of depression, fear, and anxiety. Sleep problems also occur. For long-term users, these side effects can last for days or weeks after using the drug. Another serious effect is memory loss. In a study using animals, it was shown that repeated high doses of Ecstasy caused brain damage, and this brain damage was still present six years later. It is not known yet whether the effects of Ecstasy are permanent in humans.

AMPHETAMINE AND METHAMPHETAMINE ABUSE

Amphetamine and methamphetamine are drugs that are similar to cocaine in their effects. They can be taken in pill form, or crushed and snorted. A crushed pill might also be mixed with water and injected, or smoked. Common names for amphetamines include speed, bennies, eye poppers, copilots, uppers, and black beauties. Common names for methamphetamines include meth, chalk, crank, zip, and chris. Common names for the form of methamphetamine that is smoked include ice, crystal meth, glass, and tina.

As is the case with many other street drugs, amphetamine and methamphetamine speed the release of dopamine. The large amount of dopamine provides a short-lived feeling of intense happiness. Smoking or injecting the drugs can give a high that lasts a few minutes. Users experience increased physical activity and alertness. Also, their appetite decreases while their blood pressure goes up and their heartbeat and breathing get faster. Irregular heartbeat and high body temperature are also possible side effects. Long-term use of these drugs

"I WAS TIRED OF NOBODY TRUSTING ME," BY KRYSTAN

I was adopted into a pretty good family. I played soccer a lot, but school was always a struggle for me, because I have dyslexia. At 10, I saw my brother and his friends smoking pot in the backyard. I took a couple of hits, and I felt cool. I used on weekends and hid stolen bottles of alcohol in my closet. I started smoking pot a lot more. I first tried meth when I was 13. Meth made me feel alive and alert, but also laid-back and cool.

Three weeks into sophomore year, the principal found my pipe in my locker and I got expelled. I got a misdemeanor. My parents offered me a backpacking trip in Idaho for a month. It was a wilderness camp for troubled adolescents. It turned out to be a great experience and I loved it. But as soon as I got home, I started drinking and doing meth every single day. I started stealing cash from my parents. I dropped everything: school, soccer. I was out having fun and I really didn't care.

When I was 16, I went to a dance party and afterwards wound up at some random guy's house to do dope. I wound up getting raped and beaten up outside his place. I reported it, and nothing was done. I would get hit by boyfriends. I had such low self-esteem and I thought it was normal and okay to accept the occasional smack or punch. I was lowering my standards to do anything to get dope. I didn't like myself—I felt like a monster.

My counselor told me: "You're 18. Only you can help yourself. You need to ask for help, or you need to get out of my office." I did 30 days living in a rehab clinic, another

(continues on page 70)

(continued from page 69)

30 days at a halfway house, in a sober living environment. The treatment started working for me. My clean date is June 26, 1996. Being clean and sober isn't always easy.

What means the most to me is my family's support, going to meetings, talking and sharing my story, never forgetting where I came from, how I looked, and how many people I really hurt. It means so much to have friends trust me.

Today, I'm a drug and alcohol counselor in Scotts Valley, California. You hear the horror stories, of drug users getting raped, being beaten, getting kicked out, and being homeless. If you're using and it hasn't happened to you, it's a YET.

It wasn't until I faced my life and owned up to the things I did, that my life got better. Drugs are a temporary solution to a problem. Doing drugs just makes life even harder. My life is better today thanks to the people who helped me, love me, and support me. Your life can be like that, too. Help is out there. All you have to do is ask.

Source: Reprinted with permission from Checkyourself.com, 2007.

Last name omitted by the author.

can lead to sleep difficulties, hallucinations, violent and aggressive behavior, shakes, and extreme weight loss. Methamphetamine abuse can also cause shaking and death.

LSD ABUSE

LSD, which stands for lysergic acid diethylamide, is a hallucinogen. Hallucinogens are a kind of drug that causes a person to hallucinate—to see and hear things that aren't really there. LSD is an unpredictable drug and can have very different effects on the user based on his or her personality, mood, and the environment in which the drug is taken. Other names for LSD include acid, cid, blotter, trips, tabs, barrels, and windowpane.

LSD is a powder that can take many forms. It can be taken as a pill or dissolved in liquid and put on small pieces of paper, called blotter. The paper is then chewed or swallowed to allow the drug to enter the digestive system. LSD also can be put into dried gelatin sheets, called windowpane. Sugar cubes can be sprinkled with LSD, too, and then consumed.

A use of LSD, called a trip, can have effects that last 12 hours. The physical effects of the drug include higher body temperature, increased blood pressure and heart rate, sweating, decreased appetite, shaking, large pupils, and an inability to sleep. The effects on the user's feelings and sensations are even more severe than the physical effects. The user can experience violent shifts in mood from one feeling to another. Larger doses can cause visual hallucinations, and the user's sense of time and of who he or she is might become distorted. He or she might become very frightened and panic from these experiences. Some users may fear losing control or fear death. A *bad trip* refers to a bad experience with LSD.

Users of LSD also risk having flashbacks when they are not using the drug. Flashbacks are episodes in which a sober person has feelings or sensations that are similar to a trip, even though he or she is not using LSD right then. Flashbacks can occur more than a year after using LSD.

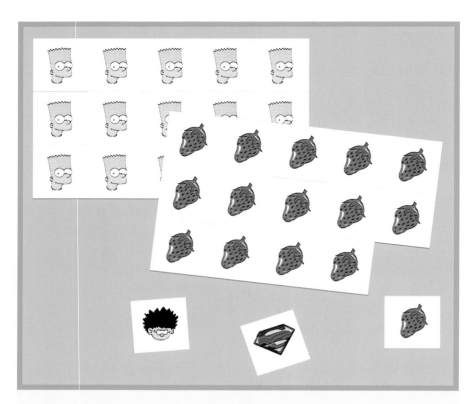

Initially developed for medical use, LSD's hallucinogenic properties can cause intense reactions relating to extreme paranoia and bad panic attacks. The drug can be sold in paper tabs featuring eye-catching designs or manufactured in dried gelatin sheets.

The drug is not considered addictive, but it can produce a tolerance. Therefore, long-term users usually increase the doses over time in an attempt to achieve the same experience they had the first time. It is with these higher doses that the more serious side effects tend to occur.

6

How Drugs Affect Users, Family, and Friends

When you use drugs, you face the possibility of becoming addicted. When someone is addicted to drugs, he or she will exhibit risky behavior in order to obtain and use drugs, and will not take into account the dangerous consequences. All that matters to that person is satisfying the addiction. That person has forgotten about everything else in life.

SCHOOL AND DRUGS

Doing well in school and doing drugs don't mix. The National Survey on Drug Use and Health (NSDUH) conducted in 2002 found that students who received grades of D or lower were much more likely to have used cigarettes, alcohol, and illegal drugs compared to students

NOWLEDGE IS POWER

School drug searches are becoming more common, despite protests from organizations and students who believe police do not have a place in an academic setting. Some people, including many school administrators, believe that the presence of police and their drug-sniffing dogs will discourage students from bringing drugs onto school grounds.

with higher grades. For example, marijuana use by students with a D average was four times that of students with an A average.

The use of drugs also has a large impact on completion of school. According to a study published in the journal, *Sociology of Education*, in 1988, high school dropouts use cigarettes and illegal drugs more than high school graduates do. And the earlier a student starts using drugs, the greater the probability that he or she will drop out of school. Statistics show that those who started using marijuana by age 13 usually did not attend college. Those who don't ever use marijuana completed, on average, almost three years of college.

FAMILIES AND DRUGS

Families can be torn apart by drugs. When parents use drugs, it affects their children. A parent who uses drugs cannot be caring toward his or her children. The basic needs of very young children—such as food and clothing—will often not be met if a parent is addicted to a drug. Many times this leads to children who are unable to act normally in social situations; for instance, they might misbehave or have trouble making friends. Children who are exposed to drugs in the home are also more likely to use drugs themselves in the future. Studies have shown that children of alcoholics are more likely to use drugs themselves, and they do worse in school compared to children of nonalcoholic parents.

Siblings have a strong influence on one another, too. A study published in the *International Journal of Addictions* in 1986 examined the influence of older brothers on younger brothers in terms of substance abuse. The older brothers had a greater influence than their parents on whether their younger brothers used drugs. If the older brother used drugs, it was more likely that the younger brother did, too. On the positive side, an older brother who did not use drugs could make up for the negative effects of parental drug use on the younger brother. According to the study, if both the older brother and friends stayed away from drugs, the younger brother was least likely to use drugs. This shows how the bonds between siblings can hurt or help a family's overall abstinence from substance abuse.

FRIENDS AND DRUGS

As previously noted, it has been shown that young people's friends influence whether they use drugs or not. Interestingly, more and more, teenagers are associating with peers who don't use drugs. According to a 2003 study from Columbia University, 56% of young people don't have any friends who drink alcohol on a regular basis, 68% don't have any friends who use marijuana, and 70% don't have any friends who smoke cigarettes. All of these figures are 4% to 14% higher than the

HOW DRUG ABUSE RELATES TO HIV

HIV is the virus that causes AIDS. HIV/AIDS attacks a person's immune system, which makes him or her at risk of catching other fatal diseases. With new treatments available today, HIV doesn't always lead to life-threatening AIDS. It has been estimated that, as of 2003, there were about one million people living with HIV or AIDS in the United States. About a quarter of the people with HIV don't know they have it.

HIV can be passed from person to person in many different ways. One of these ways is when drug users share needles. If one person is infected and shares a needle with another drug user, he or she can pass the virus to that person. And this is not the only way that HIV is linked with drug abuse. When someone uses drugs (smoking marijuana or drinking alcohol, for example) his or her mind is affected, and so is his or her judgment. Therefore, the user

previous year. It seems that young people who don't use drugs are choosing peers who have similar attitudes and values.

Also, a close-knit family situation is likely to encourage young people to avoid drugs. Often, parents who closely monitor the friends and activities of their sons and daughters end up raising children who don't use drugs. The consistent use of rules and discipline by parents has also reduced drug use among young people.

may participate in unsafe sexual activity that can put him or her at risk for contracting HIV.

You already know that drug abuse can damage a person's health in many ways. Besides affecting the brain and other organs, drugs can make the body more at risk to catching HIV. Studies have shown that HIV does more damage to the brain of a methamphetamine abuser than it does to the brain of someone who doesn't abuse drugs. Methamphetamine users who are HIV positive tend to have damage to their neurons and their cognitive ability.

Young people are particularly at risk for getting the HIV virus. A study by the Centers for Disease Control and Prevention showed that about 38,490 young people from age 13 to 24 were diagnosed with AIDS by the end of 2003. The use of drugs may be contributing to risk-taking behaviors that put them in harm's way.

FUTURE GOALS AND DRUGS

Planning and working toward a goal takes time, energy, and focus. Drugs can be a destructive force that derails your future. For one, using drugs can cause permanent damage to your body, which is a consequence you'll have to deal with for a long time. Becoming involved with drugs may also lead to dropping out of high school. Without a high school diploma, a person will earn thousands of dollars less per year in a job compared to a high school graduate. Also, a high school graduate, on average, earns about $20,000 less per year than a person with a college degree. The more education a person has, the greater his or her potential to earn more and have control over future choices and plans.

VIOLENCE AND DRUGS

A 2007 special report released by the Office of National Drug Control Policy shows that teens using drugs are more likely to be involved with violent behavior and to join gangs. The director of the ONDCP, John P. Walters, warns that people have the wrong idea about drugs such as marijuana, thought by many to be harmless. "Drug use by teenagers isn't a 'lifestyle choice' or an act of 'personal expression,'" Walters said. "It is a public health, and, increasingly, a public safety dilemma."

The ONDCP report found that:

- Marijuana is the most commonly used illegal drug among gang members.
- Young people who use marijuana are almost four times more likely to join gangs.
- Teenagers who use drugs (especially marijuana) are more likely to experiment with other drugs and steal compared to teenagers who don't use drugs.

- About 27% of teens using illegal drugs within the past year admit to attacking another individual in order to cause injury. Of the teenagers who have gotten into fights at school or work within the past year, about 17% were using drugs during that time period.
- Also, teens using marijuana on a regular basis are nine times more likely to experiment with alcohol or illegal drugs compared to teenagers who don't.
- Teenagers who don't use drugs at all function better during the difficult journey through adolescence than those who do.

THE CONSEQUENCES OF PRESCRIPTION DRUG ABUSE

The abuse of the prescription drug OxyContin by twelfth graders dropped slightly from 5.5% in 2005 to 4.3% in 2006. Nevertheless, much more needs to be done to curb the use of this highly addictive drug. Part of the problem with prescription drug abuse is that young people think it's safer because it's a prescription medication, not a street drug.

Ryan, a high school senior from Tewksbury, Massachusetts, was hooked quickly and sold most of his possessions to keep using. If he stopped using for a day or two, he would feel sick. "It was like somebody was inside of your head with a hammer," he said. "You feel like you're going to die. Just laying there in the bed, sweat pouring off of you . . . Then five minutes later, you're freezing . . . then you'd be throwing up." Ryan was scared enough by these symptoms to ask his parents for help. Others who get hooked on OxyContin don't ask for help in time.

MADD ABOUT DRUNK DRIVING

On the night of October 13, 2000, Ruth and John McCarthy were driving home when their car was struck by another car. The other driver, Douglas Lamond, had drunk too much alcohol to drive, and he was speeding and talking on his cell phone at the time of the crash. The McCarthys both had life-threatening injuries from the crash, and Ruth McCarthy died. The following week, Ruth and John were to celebrate their fiftieth wedding anniversary.

Ruth left behind her husband, John, and her four grown children, Billinda, Kevin, Greg, and Jenn. Ruth's death and John's injuries were devastating, and the situation deeply affected the family. Everyone coped with Ruth's death in different and very personal ways.

Jenn McCarthy decided to channel the power of her grief and anger by taking part in a public mission to combat drunk driving. She joined a Connecticut chapter of Mothers Against Drunk Driving (MADD). Between 2003 and 2007, Jenn raised more than $10,000 to support MADD's campaign against drunk driving, and she continues to help. One of the annual fund-raising events she takes part in is a MADD walkathon, which she participates in with her husband, Chuck, and two sons, Asher and Caven. Friends and relatives sponsor her as she walks in the memory of her mother.

For her dedication to MADD's mission to stop drunk driving, Jenn was honored with the organization's Community Service Award. In addition, she received an official citation of congratulations from Connecticut Attorney General Richard Blumenthal in recognition of her

Jenn McCarthy took a stand in support of Mothers Against Drunk Driving (MADD) after her mother died in a car accident involving a driver who was under the influence. Her valuable community service work was recognized with an award from Connecticut Attorney General Richard Bluementhal *(left)*.

work. With passion and memories of her mother always in her thoughts, Jenn continues to combat drunk driving, and perhaps to prevent more innocent deaths.

Douglas Lamond was at first charged with second-degree manslaughter, but was only convicted of misconduct with a motor vehicle and operating under the influence, both of which are much less serious crimes. He ended up serving four months in prison and serving five years of probation. During his probation, Lamond was ordered by the court to speak to school children about the consequences of drunk driving, perform 100 hours of community service, and serve on a Mothers Against Drunk Driving Victim's Impact Panel. It was not as lengthy a sentence as the McCarthy family had expected, but they hope it might allow them to begin healing.

Christopher Oates, who was the captain of his football and wrestling teams, experimented with another prescription drug, Percocet, after his doctor prescribed it to him for a football injury. Chris experimented with Percocet and then moved on to OxyContin. While using Oxycontin with friends, Christopher was hooked. He then moved from using the expensive OxyContin (about $80 per pill) to the cheaper heroin (about five dollars per bag). Christopher died at age 19 from a heroin overdose. The night before he died, he and his mother talked until three the next morning about his problem. According to his mother, Cheryl, he said he knew he needed help. She says that he "got grabbed by something that was greater than him." Cheryl Oates recommends that parents lock up all prescription medications to keep them away from teenagers looking to experiment with drugs.

7

How to Handle Drug Use and Abuse

You have read a great deal about the dangers of drugs. Knowing what kind of damage they can do to your body and your life, how would you deal with a situation in which drugs are offered to you? What do you do to deal with peer pressure? Here are some ways to handle difficult situations that involve helping yourself or others deal with drugs.

HELP YOURSELF AND AVOID PEER PRESSURE

Eating well and staying physically active through sports or other activities goes a long way toward helping you feel healthy. Staying healthy also involves keeping harmful chemicals, such as drugs, out of your body. Setting short and long-term goals for what you want to accomplish or do in the future helps you take steps toward achieving dreams you have, which helps you feel good mentally. Having good relationships with your family members and friends builds a network to support you and help you mature as a person.

Yet, not everyone has a clear idea of what is healthy and of what the best kind of support is to give a friend or family member. For example, a person might offer drugs to his friend because he or she thinks it's the normal thing to do, and that it's fun. He or she might not realize the true consequences of drug use. So if a friend starts offering you drugs, how are you supposed to deal with that? How do you fight peer pressure?

Peer pressure can come in two forms: positive and negative. Positive peer pressure is pressure that someone feels to do something healthy or productive. An example of positive peer pressure is encouraging a friend to try out for a sports team, or to not drink and drive. The result or consequence of positive peer pressure benefits the person being "pressured." Negative peer pressure, on the other hand, has a negative consequence. Peer pressure to steal or do drugs is negative peer pressure. The consequence of negative peer pressure is destructive to the person being pressured.

When dealing with negative peer pressure to take drugs, it is important to know why peer pressure exists. It is likely that most people feel some pressure to belong to a group. This is a common feeling among people because membership in a group means a person is surrounded and supported by others. A friend who offers you drugs might have accepted an offer of drugs by another friend, and accepted it just because he or she wanted to belong. Being accepted by a group can give you a sense of confidence and can make you feel happy to belong. However, if that group turns out to be the

The results of positive peer pressure can come from strong relationships and safe activities. Being a part of a sports team, for example, encourages closer friendships that can lead people to encourage others to focus on their skills and abilities rather than substances that lead to addiction.

wrong kind of crowd for you, it may be difficult to separate yourself from them—even if you don't agree with the group's choice to do drugs or other harmful things.

You must make your own choices regardless of what the group does. Knowing the facts about drugs and the dangers of taking them can help strengthen your decision. You and your loved ones have to live with the consequences of your taking drugs, both immediately and in the long-term.

The best way to turn down drugs is to keep it low-key. You can politely decline and say, "no, thanks," without making a big deal of it. If these people are really your friends, they won't be too insistent about having you use drugs with them. By playing it low-key, you avoid starting an argument with your friends by being aggressive about it, while at the same time making a decision for yourself. It's possible that other friends may take notice of the way you handled the situation and they may think twice about using drugs the next time.

There are other responses that you can use when a friend offers you drugs:

- If you are involved in sports, you could tell your friends that you are in training and can't afford to use drugs.
- Explain that you have better ways to use your time than to do drugs.
- Explain that the possible consequences of getting arrested and disappointing your family aren't worth it.
- Explain that it will hurt your brain cells, and joke that you need every brain cell you've got.

If you notice that your group of friends is using drugs more and more frequently, you may decide to decrease the time you spend with them. It might get more difficult or uncomfortable to say no each time. You may have to spend more time with friends you have who share more similar interests with you. This doesn't mean you shouldn't try to help a friend who you think has developed a drug problem, though.

HELPING A FRIEND

Helping a friend who is using drugs can be a difficult and frustrating undertaking. But you may be the first, or only, person who knows what is going on in your friend's life. You can make all the difference. This friend is most likely experiencing the same kind of negative peer pressure that you might experience, too. The best time to help this friend is when he or she is sober and not with the rest of the group. When the rest of the group is around, your friend might not feel comfortable talking to you openly. Consider the following steps.

Begin by thinking through what you're going to say and how you're going to say it. Sit down with your friend in a place where you have privacy to talk. Talk in a calm but serious tone about your concerns. Discuss any changes you have seen in his or her behavior that worry you. Try not to sound judgmental, just concerned about what you see. Take time to listen to how your friend responds. He or she may not be ready to discuss this issue, or even to recognize the problem.

If he or she denies the problem, it is important that you continue the discussion at a later time. Keep up a connection and repeat how you are there to help and support that person. Talk to supportive adults in the person's life—such as parents, counselors, or coaches—to get their perspective on the situation. This is a stressful situation for you as well, and getting support from others could help a great deal.

If you don't see any improvement in the situation over time, you may need to limit your time with your friend. You want to help your friend, but keep in mind that you are putting yourself at risk by spending time with someone who uses drugs. Keep your connection with family and other friends and continue to be involved in healthy activities.

HELPING A SIBLING

Helping a sibling with a drug problem can start with a conversation similar to the one you might have with a friend. Express your concern and worry over his or her health. Your parents should be involved at some point, too. They have a right to know what is going on. But first, it is important to begin and maintain a conversation with your sibling about the issue.

When it is time to speak to your parents, talk to them alone at first, so that the shock and anger they express over the situation doesn't scare away your sibling. You don't want to undo any progress you might have made in getting him or her to discuss the problem. Together, as a supportive family, you can help your sibling progress through treatment.

TREATMENT FOR DRUG ADDICTION

Drug addiction is considered a kind of disease and is treated as one. Remember, when someone is addicted to a drug, he or she will seek out drugs at any cost or consequence. The addicted person must go through treatment to address the behavioral issues that brought about the addiction, as well as the physical symptoms.

Drug addiction treatment for long-term users doesn't always succeed without one or more relapses—instances in which they fall back into drug use. But over time and with consistent treatment, the individual may lead a productive, drug-free life. Unfortunately, not everyone who needs treatment gets it. In 2004, only 3.8 million people received drug addiction treatment out of the 22.5

million people aged 12 or older in the United States who needed it.

According to research, there are key pieces to an effective drug treatment program. Treatment must be molded to meet the many needs of each patient, not just the drug addiction. The physical and mental needs of the patient must be considered when developing each person's counseling and behavior therapies. Effective treatment also requires a lot of time to get the patient back to health, and it is an amount of time that also varies widely among individuals.

Treatment often begins with detoxifying the patient. This means that the patient stops use of the drug to cleanse the body. During this time the patient will go through withdrawal. Because the brain of a drug addict has adjusted to having the drug present, it works differently when use of the drugs is stopped. Symptoms of withdrawal can include intense chills, shaking, fever, body aches, sweating, and vomiting. Treatment centers are now using medications to treat these symptoms and the drug cravings that also happen during withdrawal. Medications such as buprenorphine can help by acting on the parts of the brain upon which the drug once acted. The medication blocks the action of the drug and the withdrawal symptoms, and helps relieve cravings for the drug.

After detoxification, some type of behavioral treatment occurs. Behavioral treatment tries to change the drug user's attitudes and behaviors regarding drugs. It can occur through individual or group therapy sessions. Different types of therapy focus on helping patients understand why they used drugs and how to avoid putting themselves in situations in which they would use again. Family therapy can be used when the drug user is an adolescent.

People battling substance addictions often take part in group therapy sessions, in which they can talk about their problems with drugs or alcohol.

These therapies can happen as part of residential treatment or outpatient treatment. Residential treatment is when the patient lives at the treatment facility. There are programs called therapeutic communities (TCs) that provide a structured environment for the patient for up to 12 months. Patients who reside in TCs are often those who have used drugs for long periods of time or have participated in criminal activities. Outpatient treatment is when the patient makes regular visits to a treatment facility but does not live there.

According to 2003 statistics collected by the U.S. Department of Health and Human Services, about 23% of the 1.7 million people who entered treatment facilities entered for help with alcohol abuse. Marijuana abuse, the largest percentage among illegal drugs, contributed to about 15% of the total treatment center admissions. Heroin abuse accounted for about 14% of the total admissions.

The three largest groups of admissions were Caucasians (about 62%), African-Americans (about 24%), and Hispanics/Latinos (about 13%). The remaining admissions were made up of American Indians, Alaskan Natives, Asian Americans, Hawaiians, and Pacific Islanders. The largest age group of admissions was 36 to 40 years old (about 16%). In comparison, the age group 12 to 17 years old made up about 9% of the 1.7 million admissions.

LOCATING TREATMENT FACILITIES

One very useful resource provided by the government is through the Substance Abuse and Mental Health Services Administration (SAMHSA). The SAMHSA Web site provides a search tool to find a treatment facility. The search tool is called the Substance Abuse Treatment Facility Locator and it can be found at http://findtreatment. samhsa.gov. There is also a phone number that can be used to get help finding treatment. The phone number is 1–800–662-HELP.

PHOENIX HOUSE

Phoenix House is the country's largest nonprofit substance abuse treatment and prevention center. In 2007, the organization celebrated its fortieth year of helping men, women, and teenagers reestablish drug-free lives. Phoenix House has more than 100 programs across the country and treats about 6,000 men, women, and teenagers daily.

Phoenix House uses residential treatment to help its patients. Programs are located in New York, California, Texas, Florida, and throughout New England. Throughout

In 1967, six heroin addicts in New York decided to give up drugs and help each other stay clean by living together and supporting one another. The community they built became known as Phoenix House, and it is now the largest drug treatment and prevention center in the United States. As the organization has expanded, it has helped thousands of people with substance abuse problems and garnered the financial and social support of celebrities, such as actor and comedian George Lopez *(right)* and singer Lorna Luft *(left).*

its 40 years of practice, Phoenix House has helped more than 150,000 people with their substance abuse problems. It was the first such organization to include the role of family in preventing and treating substance abuse. Phoenix House also established the "Academy" so that teenagers could continue their education during treatment. Patients are also active with community organizations to learn new skills and the confidence that empower them in their lives.

EDUCATION IS KEY

The large variety of treatment options makes it possible for different people—of all personality types and backgrounds—to stop using drugs. Educating yourself and others about drugs and these treatment options is the best way to make the right choices.

GLOSSARY

Addiction   An intense craving for a substance that results in the person, or addict, going to extreme lengths to obtain and use the substance. Often addiction takes place without concern over one's health or others.

Alcoholism   A disorder that causes a person to drink alcohol in large quantities, characterized by a psychological and physical dependence on alcohol

Anabolic steroids   Human-made hormones used to help bodily tissues grow, and which are sometimes abused by athletes to increase the size and strength of their muscles and to improve endurance

Blood transfusion   The act of transferring blood into a person's blood vessels

Cocaine   A drug taken from coca leaves that is used in medicine to reduce pain and used illegally to experience a high

Controlled substance   A substance that is considered harmful and restricted by law

Crystal methamphetamine   A drug developed from amphetamine that is often used illegally to stimulate the central nervous system

Ecstasy   An illegal drug that stimulates the brain and causes hallucinations. Its scientific name is methylenedioxymethamphetamine, or MDMA.

Euphoria   A strong feeling of happiness

Hallucination   The experience of seeing, hearing, touching, and/or smelling things that are not really there, usually as the result of taking a drug that causes this effect

Heroin   An addictive drug made from the opium poppy

High   A state of being impaired by a drug

Hit   A single dose of a recreational drug

HIV/AIDS   HIV stands for human immunodeficiency virus; it is a virus that infects and destroys the immune system. AIDS stands for acquired immunodeficiency syndrome; it is a disease of the human immune system that causes a person to be vulnerable to life-threatening diseases.

Marijuana Dried leaves and flowering tops of the female hemp plant, usually used illegally as a recreational drug

Crystal methamphetamine A drug developed from amphetamine that is often used illegally to stimulate the central nervous system

Morals Personal set of rules about what is right or wrong

Narcotic A drug that dulls the senses, relieves pain, and causes sleepiness, but can have dangerous effects when taken in large doses

Nicotine A drug found in tobacco that acts to increase heart and breathing rates

Opiate A drug made from opium that tends to cause sleep and relieve pain

Opioids A human-made drug made to resemble an opiate

Overdose Too great a dose; a lethal or toxic amount

OxyContin A narcotic drug used to treat moderate to severe pain

Peer pressure A positive or negative influence from another person who is of one's age group

Performance-enhancing drug A substance taken to increase a particular physical skill

Physical dependence A state in which a person's body comes to rely on the presence of a drug or medication after long-term use

Side effect A usually negative consequence of using a substance

Stimulant A type of substance, such as a drug, that briefly increases the activity of the body and brain

Stroke A sudden decrease or loss of consciousness, sensation, and voluntary movement caused by the rupture or blockage of a blood vessel in the brain

Substance abuse   The misuse of a substance that is considered to be harmful and that is usually legally restricted

Testosterone   A natural chemical made in the body that causes the development of certain male characteristics

Tobacco   A tall tropical American herb grown for its leaves, which are prepared for smoking, chewing, or used as snuff

Withdrawal   The process of giving up an addictive drug after long-term use of it. Stopping use of a drug often brings on physical symptoms that can include nausea, sweating, and/ or depression.

BIBLIOGRAPHY

Appel, Adrianne. "Drug-Sniffing Wasps May Sting Crooks." National Geographic News, October 27, 2005. Available online. URL: http://news.nationalgeographic.com/news/2005/10/1027_051027_bombsniffwasps.html. Accessed June 7, 2007.

Arnold, Chris. "Teen Abuse of Painkiller OxyContin on the Rise." National Public Radio, May 30, 2007. Available online. URL: http://www.npr.org/templates/story/story.php?storyId=5061674. Accessed May 30, 2007.

Associated Press. "Alabama Woman on Horseback Charged with DUI." April 4, 2007. Available online. URL: http://www.msnbc.msn.com/id/17953259. Accessed April 6, 2007.

Associated Press. "Eric Clapton Rethinks Playing 'Cocaine.'" October 3, 2006. Available online. URL: http://www.breitbart.com/article.php?id=D8KH7LK81&show_article=1. Accessed July 30, 2007.

Associated Press. "Pro wrestling to institute random drug testing." December 4, 2005. Available online. URL: http://sports.espn.go.com/espn/news/story?id=2248346. Accessed July 26, 2007.

Atkinson, John S., Alan J. Richard, and Jerry W. Carlson. "The Influence of Peer, Family, and School Relationships in Substance Use Among Participation in a Youth Jobs Program." *Journal of Child & Adolescent Substance Abuse* 11 (2001): 45–54.

Barrett, Ted. "McGwire mum on steroids in hearing." March 17, 2005. Available online. URL: http://www.cnn.com/2005/ALLPOLITICS/03/17/steroids.baseball. Accessed July 22, 2007.

Blue Cross/Blue Shield. "Blue Cross/Blue Shield Says 1.1 Million Teens Have Used Performance Enhancing Sports Supplements and Drugs." October 31, 2003. Available online. URL: http://www.supplementquality.com/news/ephedra_teens_BCBS.html. Accessed July 15, 2007.

Brook, J.S., M. Whiteman, A.S. Gordon, and D.W. Brook. "The role of older brothers in younger brothers' drug use viewed in the context of parent and peer influences." *Journal of Genetic Psychology* 151 (1990): 59–75.

Christoffersen, John. "WWE suspends 10 wrestlers for violating policy on steroids and other drugs." August 31, 2007. Available online. URL: http://news.yahoo.com/s/ap/20070831/ap_en_tv/steroid_raid_wrestlers. Accessed August 31, 2007.

Clark, Ryan. "Breaking News: 11 Wrestlers Named in Steroid Probe." March 19, 2007. Available online. URL: http://www.wrestlinginc.com/v2/wi/stc/nws/2007/3/19/23008.shtml. Accessed July 27, 2007.

Dalton, Madeline A., James D. Sargent, Michael L. Beach, et al. "Effect of viewing smoking in movies on adolescent smoking initiation: a cohort study." *The Lancet* 362 (2003): 281–285.

Davis, Wade, and Andrew Weil. "Bufo alvarius: A Potent Hallucinogen of Animal Origin." *Journal of Ethnopharmacology* 41 (1994): 1–8.

Difilippo, Dana. "How drugs harm the family tree." *Philadelphia Daily News*, June 11, 2007. Available online. URL: http://www.philly.com/dailynews/local/20070611_HOW_DRUGS_HARM_THE_FAMILY_TREE.html. Accessed July 11, 2007.

Dotinga, Randy. "U.S. Kids Have Watched Stars Smoking Billions of Times." May 7, 2007. Available online. URL: http://health.msn.com/guides/stopsmoking/articlepage.aspx?cp-documentid=100162593. Accessed May 15, 2007.

Freevibe. "Media Hype." Available online. URL: http://www.freevibe.com/Drug_Facts/media_hype.asp. Accessed July 25, 2007.

Gambrell, Jon. "Drink Mix Makes Its Way into Meth." *The Press-Telegram*, May 1, 2007. Available online. URL: http://www.presstelegram.com/news/ci_5796230. Accessed May 8, 2007.

Handwerk, Brian. "'Detector Dogs' Sniff Out Smugglers for U.S. Customs." National Geographic News, July 12, 2002. Available online. URL: http://news.nationalgeographic. com/news/2002/07/0712_020712_drugdogs.html. Accessed June 7, 2007.

Hardcastle, Mark. "Teen Advice Teen Life Drug & Alcohol FAQ." Available online. URL: http://teenadvice.about.com/ cs/teenlifefaqs/a/drugalcoholFAQ.htm. Accessed November 27, 2007.

Hartstein, Larry, and Todd Holcomb. "Drug testing by high schools gets a push from QB's death: The debate has begun: Some high schools see it as an invasion of privacy, but others wonder if programs could help prevent another tragedy." *The Atlanta Journal-Constitution*, July 10, 2007, news section.

Holcomb, Todd. "Debate rages on steroid testing: Make it mandatory? High school officials say tests are warranted, but the high cost scares off most programs." *The Atlanta Journal-Constitution*, June 12, 2007, sports section.

Hyphantis, T., V. Koutras, A. Liakos, and M. Marselos. "Alcohol and drug use, family situation and school performance in adolescent children of alcoholics." *International Journal of Social Psychiatry* 37 (1991): 35–42.

Jones, Richard Lezin. "New Jersey Plans Broad Steroids Testing for School Sports." *New York Times*, December 21, 2005. Available online. URL: http://www.nytimes. com/2005/12/21/sports/othersports/21steroids.html?ex= 1292821200&en=f17f5d621b0de38b&ei=5088&partner= rssnyt&emc=rss. Accessed July 17, 2007.

Keifer, Michael. "Ex-wife says cocaine habit killed baseball star." *The Arizona Republic*, August 1, 2007. Available online. URL: http://www.azcentral.com/arizonarepublic/ news/articles/0801beck0801.html. Accessed August 15, 2007.

Kennedy, Tracy. "New Hartford man gets 120 days in death." *The Register Citizen*, February 25, 2005. Available online.

URL: http://www.registercitizen.com/site/index.cfm?
newsid=14032820&BRD=1652&PAG=461&dept_id=
12530&rfi=8. Accessed July 2, 2007.

Kesteloot, Hugo. "Queen Margrethe II and mortality in
Danish women." *The Lancet* 357 (2001): 871–872.

Kids' Health. "What You Need to Know About Drugs." Available online. URL: http://www.kidshealth.org/kid/grow/
drugs_alcohol/know_drugs.html. Accessed February 2,
2007.

Meadows, Michelle. "Prescription Drug Use and Abuse." *U.S.
Food and Drug Administration Consumer Magazine*, September 2001. Available online. URL: http://www.fda.gov/fdac/
features/2001/501_drug.html. Accessed May 30, 2007.

Mensch, Barbara S., and Denise B. Kandel. "Dropping out of
high school and drug involvement." *Sociology of Education*
61 (1988): 95–113.

Mothers Against Drunk Driving. "Alcohol-related laws."
Available online. URL: http://www.madd.org/laws/law.
Accessed January 1, 2007.

National Center for Educational Statistics. "Median annual
earnings of full-time, full-year wage and salary workers
ages 25–34, by race/ethnicity and educational attain-
ment: Selected years, 1980–2005." Available online. URL:
http://nces.ed.gov/programs/coe/2007/section2/table.
asp?tableID=696. Accessed July 22, 2007.

National Center on Addiction and Substance Abuse. "CASA
2003 Teen Survey: High Stress, Frequent Boredom, Too
Much Spending Money: Triple Threat that Hikes Risk of
Teen Substance Abuse." Available online. URL: http://www.
casacolumbia.org/absolutenm/templates/PressReleases.aspx
?articleid=348&zoneid=46. Accessed April 6, 2007.

National Clearinghouse for Alcohol and Drug Information.
"Alcohol and Drug Use Influence Academic Performance."
Available online. URL: http://ncadi.samhsa.gov/newsroom/
rep/2005/academics_alcohol.aspx. Accessed July 20, 2007.

National Drug Strategy Network. "Secretions From Colorado Toad Contain Powerful Psychedelic Compound." Available online. URL: http://ndsn.org.july94.html. Accessed July 17, 2007.

National Institute on Drug Abuse. "InfoFacts: Crack and Cocaine." Available online. URL: http://www.drugabuse. gov/Infofacts/cocaine.html. Accessed June 21, 2007.

National Institute on Drug Abuse. "InfoFacts: Ecstasy." Available online. URL: http://www.drugabuse.gov/Infofacts/ ecstasy.html. Accessed June 21, 2007.

National Institute on Drug Abuse. "InfoFacts: Heroin." Available online. URL: http://www.drugabuse.gov/Infofacts/ heroin.html. Accessed June 22, 2007.

National Institute on Drug Abuse. "InfoFacts: High School and Youth Trends." Available online. URL: http://www. drugabuse.gov/Infofacts/HSYouthtrends.html. Accessed January 16, 2007.

National Institute on Drug Abuse. "InfoFacts: LSD." Available online. URL: http://www.drugabuse.gov/Infofacts/lsd.html. Accessed June 25, 2007.

National Institute on Drug Abuse. "InfoFacts: Marijuana." Available online. URL: http://www.nida.nih.gov/Infofacts/ marijuana.html. Accessed June 20, 2007.

National Institute on Drug Abuse. "InfoFacts: Methamphetamine." Available online. URL: http://www.drugabuse.gov/ Infofacts/methamphetamine.html. Accessed June 25, 2007.

National Institute on Drug Abuse. "InfoFacts: Prescription Pain and Other Medications." Available online. URL: http://www.drugabuse.gov/Infofacts/PainMed.html. Accessed June 7, 2007.

National Institute on Drug Abuse. "InfoFacts: Steroids." Available online. URL: http://www.drugabuse.gov/Infofacts/ steroids.html. Accessed June 25, 2007.

National Institute on Drug Abuse. "InfoFacts: Treatment Approaches for Drug Addiction." Available online. URL:

http://www.drugabuse.gov/Infofacts/TreatMeth.html. Accessed June 25, 2007.

National Institute on Drug Abuse. "InfoFacts: Treatment Trends." Available online. URL: http://www.drugabuse. gov/Infofacts/treatmenttrends.html. Accessed January 16, 2007.

National Institute on Drug Abuse. "Marijuana: Facts for Teens." Available online. URL: http://www.drugabuse.gov/ MarijBroch/Marijteenstxt.html. Accessed June 20, 2007.

National Institute on Drug Abuse. "Marijuana Smoking Is Associated With a Spectrum of Respiratory Disorders." Available online. URL: http://www.drugabuse.gov/NIDA_ notes/NNvol21N1/Marijuana.html. Accessed January 16, 2007.

National Institute on Drug Abuse. "NIDA Community Drug Alert Bulletin: Club Drugs." Available online. URL: http://www.drugabuse.gov/ClubAlert/ClubdrugAlert.html. Accessed June 25, 2007.

National Institute on Drug Abuse. "Relationships Matter: Impact of Parental, Peer Factors on Teen, Young Adult Substance Abuse." Available online. URL: http://www. drugabuse.gov/NIDA_notes/NNvol18N2/Relationships. html. Accessed July 14, 2007.

National Institute on Drug Abuse for Teens. "Anabolic Steroids." Available online. URL: http://www.teens.drugabuse. gov/facts/facts_ster1.asp. Accessed January 16, 2007.

National Institute on Drug Abuse for Teens. "Ecstasy." Available online. URL: http://www.teens.drugabuse.gov/facts/ facts_xtc1.asp. Accessed January 16, 2007.

National Institute on Drug Abuse for Teens. "HIV/AIDS." Available online. URL: http://www.teens.drugabuse.gov/ facts/facts_hiv1.asp. Accessed January 16, 2007.

National Institute on Drug Abuse for Teens. "Inhalants." Available online. URL: http://www.teens.drugabuse.gov/ facts/facts_inhale1.asp. Accessed January 16, 2007.

National Institute on Drug Abuse for Teens. "Marijuana."
Available online. URL: http://www.teens.drugabuse.gov/
facts/facts_mj1.asp. Accessed January 16, 2007.

National Institute on Drug Abuse for Teens. "Nicotine."
Available online. URL: http://www.teens.drugabuse.gov/
facts/facts_nicotine1.asp. Accessed January 16, 2007.

National Institute on Drug Abuse for Teens. "Stimulants."
Available online. URL: http://www.teens.drugabuse.gov/
facts/facts_stim1.asp. Accessed January 16, 2007.

Needle, R., H. McCubbin, M. Wilson, R. Reinbeck, A. Lazar,
and H. Mederer. "Interpersonal influences in adolescent
drug use: the role of older siblings, parents, and peers."
International Journal of Addiction 21 (1986): 739–766.

Neuroscience for Kids. "Alcohol and the Brain." Available
online. URL: http://faculty.washington.edu/chudler/alco.
html. Accessed January 17, 2007.

Neuroscience for Kids. "Amphetamines." Available online.
URL: http://faculty.washington.edu/chudler/amp.html.
Accessed June 25, 2007.

Neuroscience for Kids. "Cocaine." Available online. URL:
http://faculty.washington.edu/chudler/coca.html. Accessed
January 18, 2007.

Neuroscience for Kids. "Heroin." Available online. URL:
http://faculty.washington.edu/chudler/hero.html. Accessed
January 17, 2007.

Neuroscience for Kids. "Marijuana." Available online. URL:
http://faculty.washington.edu/chudler/mari.html. Accessed
January 18, 2007.

Office of National Drug Control Policy. "Doping." Available
online. URL: http://www.whitehousedrugpolicy.gov/
prevent/sports/doping.html. Accessed July 20, 2007.

Office of National Drug Control Policy. "Early Marijuana Use
a Warning Sign For Later Gang Involvement." Available
online. URL: http://www.mediacampaign.org/newsroom/
press07/061907html. Accessed July 30, 2007.

Office of National Drug Control Policy. "The Economic Cost of Drug Abuse in the United States." Available online. URL: http://www.whitehousedrugpolicy.gov/publications/pdf/economic_costs98.pdf. Accessed January 16, 2007.

Phoenix House. "Phoenix House Celebrates 40 Years of Saving Lives." Available online. URL: http://www.phoenixhouse.org/California/WhatsNew/PressReleases/40YearAnniversary.html. Accessed August 15, 2007.

Planas, Antonio. "High school drug testing promoted." *Las Vegas Review-Journal*, April 25, 2007. Available online. URL: http://www.lvrj.com/news/7183316.html. Accessed July 19, 2007.

Richey, Warren. "Court Expands School Drug Tests." *The Christian Science Monitor*, June 28, 2002. Available online. URL: http://www.csmonitor.com/2002/0628/p01s01-usju.html. Accessed July 18, 2007.

Sargent, J.D., T.A. Wills, M. Stoolmiller, J. Gibson, and F.X. Gibbons. "Alcohol use in motion pictures and its relation with early-onset teen drinking." *Journal of Studies on Alcohol* 67 (2006): 54–65.

The Site. "Peer Pressure." Available online. URL: http://www.thesite.org/drinkanddrugs/drugsafety/usingdrugs/peerpressure Accessed January 15, 2007.

Sovndal, Shannon. "The Hamilton Case: A doctor explains blood doping." September 28, 2004. Available online. URL: http://www.velonews.com/news/fea/7027.0.html.

StraightWay Drug Prevention. "The StraightWay Team." Available online. URL: http://www.straightway.org/index.htm. Accessed July 27, 2007.

Substance Abuse and Mental Health Services Administration. "Synar Amendment." Available online. URL: http://prevention.samhsa.gov/tobacco/default.aspx. Accessed January 1, 2007.

Swartz, Jon. "High death rate lingers behind fun facade of pro wrestling." *USA Today*, March 12, 2004. Available online. URL: http://www.usatoday.com/sports/2004-03-12-pro-wrestling_x.htm. Accessed July 26, 2007.

Thompson, K.M., and F. Yokota. "Depiction of alcohol, tobacco, and other substances in G-rated animated feature films." *Pediatrics* 107 (2001): 1369–1374.

The Times of India. "Scorpion Sting for Addicts in South Gujarat." April 29, 2003. Available online. URL: http://timesofindia.indiatimes.com/articleshow/msid-44894466,prtpage-1.cms. Accessed June 17, 2007.

Trahan, Jason. "Danger of 'Cheese' Lies in Teens' Perception." *The Dallas Morning News*, March 9, 2007. Available online. URL: http://www.phoenixhouse.org/Content/WhatsNew/PHintheNews/images/popups/2006/Dallas%20Morning%20News%203–9-07%20Cheese.pdf. Accessed July 1, 2007.

U.S. Drug Enforcement Administration. "Controlled Substances Act." Available online. URL: http://www.dea.gov/pubs/csa.html. Accessed January 1, 2007.

U.S. Department of Health and Human Services. "Role Models at Family Guide." Available online. URL: http://family.samhsa.gov/be/rolemodel.aspx. Accessed January 14, 2007.

U.S. Department of Health and Human Services. "Center for Substance Abuse Treatment Advisory: OxyContin: Prescription Drug Abuse." Available online. URL: http://ncadi.samhsa.gov/govpubs/ms726. Accessed May 30, 2007.

Varghese, S.T., Y. Balhara, and A. Mondal. "Unconventional Substances of Abuse: Scorpions and Lizards." *Journal of Postgraduate Medicine*, 2006. Available online. URL: http://www.jpgmonline.com/text.asp?2006/52/4/325/28170. Accessed July 6, 2007.

Walker, Ben. "Drug Tie In Baseball Star's Death." CBS News, November 1, 2004. Available online. URL: http://www.cbsnews.com/stories/2004/10/11/entertainment/main648472.shtml. Accessed July 26, 2007.

Wescott, Scott. "One Community Leader's Quest to Fight Meth." The Partnership for a Drug-Free American, July 5,

2006. Available online. URL: http://www.drugfree.org/ Portal/DrugIssue/MethResources/one_community_leader. html. Accessed July 27, 2007.

White, Jerry, and Andrew Curry. "Tainted Tour de France finishes under cloud." *The Christian Science Monitor*, July 30, 2007, World section.

Winstead Journal. "MADD Honors Local Resident." Available online. URL: http://www.tcextra.com/news/publish/ barkhamsted/MADD_Honors_Local_Resident/4400.shtml. Accessed July 26, 2007.

Yamaguchi, Ryoko, Lloyd D. Johnston, and Patrick M. O'Malley. "Relationship Between Student Illicit Drug Use and School Drug-Testing Policies." *Journal of School Health* 73 (2003): 159–164.

FURTHER READING

Apel, Melanie. *Cocaine and Your Nose: The Incredibly Disgusting Story.* New York: Rosen Publishing Group, 2000.

Cobb, Allan B. *Heroin and Your Veins: The Incredibly Disgusting Story.* New York: Rosen Publishing Group, 2000.

Esherick, Joan. *Dying for Acceptance: A Teen's Guide to Drug- and Alcohol-Related Health Issues.* Broomall, Penn.: Mason Crest Publishers, 2004.

Phillips, Jane Ellen. *LSD, PCP & Other Hallucinogens.* New York: Chelsea House Publishers, 2000.

Stanley, Debbie. *Marijuana and Your Lungs: The Incredibly Disgusting Story.* New York: Rosen Publishing Group, 2000.

Werther, Scott P. *Ecstasy and Your Heart: The Incredibly Disgusting Story.* New York: Rosen Publishing Group, 2000.

WEB SITES

TEEN DRUG ABUSE

http://www.teen-drug-abuse.org

This site provides useful information about drugs and treatment centers. There are also links to drug-related news stories.

DRUG FREE AMERICA FOUNDATION

http://www.dfaf.org

The Drug Free America Foundation is an organization that provides information about various drugs and issues surrounding their use. Included in the student section of this Web site are suggestions on how to talk to a parent about drugs.

CHECKYOURSELF.ORG

http://checkyourself.org

This is the teen site for the Partnership for a Drug-Free America. Included on it are self-quizzes about drugs, drug information, a glossary, and stories shared by teens who have had drug problems.

PHOTO CREDITS

INDEX

A

addiction
history, 6
physical dependence *vs.*, 58
psychological, 64
advertising, 30
Alabama Autauga County
schools, 20
alcohol
abuse, 47–49, 80–81
age and, 13–14
cost to society, 19
effects, 48–49
mixing cocaine with, 65
movies and, 29
overview, 47–48
signs of use, 48
in songs, 24–25
treatment for abuse, 90
use by adolescents, 17
amphetamine abuse, 68, 70
anabolic steroids
health impacts, 32, 34,
55–56
overview, 55
sports and, 32
testing in schools for, 18
use by adolescents, 17
animals, 15–16

B

baseball, 35–36
Beck, Rodney, 35–36
blood transfusions, 32–34
boredom, 23
Bush, George W., 34–35, 41

C

caffeine, 34
Cage, Nicolas, 29
Caminiti, Ken, 35
chain smoking, 26
"cheese," 22
cigarettes
nicotine absorption, 50
use by adolescents, 17
use by role models, 26, 27, 29
Clapton, Eric, 25
Coca-Cola, 6
cocaine
abuse, 64–65
detecting, 16

health impact, 19–20, 34, 35
history of use, 6–7
"Cocaine" (song, Clapton), 25
costs
of drug abuse, 8, 19
of drug testing in schools, 18
of treatment centers, 8
crack. *See* cocaine
crimes, drug-related, 19
cycling, 35

D

D.A.R.E. (Drug Abuse Resistance
Education), 9, 10–11, 42
deaths
from cocaine, 19–20, 35
from heroin, 82
of sports stars, 35–36
from steroids, 32
detoxification, 89
dogs, drug-sniffing, 16
dopamine, 50, 64, 68
doping, 30, 32–36
Drug Enforcement Administration
(DEA), 7
drug mixtures, 22, 57, 65
Drug War, 7
drugs
defined, 12–13
reasons for using, 21–23
refusing, 38–39, 86–87
signs of using, 22
social norms and, 14
drunk driving, 80–81

E

Ecstasy, 66–68
education
D.A.R.E., 9, 10–11, 42
information sources, 37,
40–41
"Just Say No," 8
endorphins, 66
ethanol, 47
ethnic groups and treatment, 91

F

families and drug use, 75, 77, 88
flashbacks, 71
Ford, Betty, 8
Fourth Amendment, 18
friends, helping drug-using, 87–88

G
gangs, 78
Guerrero, Eddie, 32–33

H
hallucinogens
    animal and insect venom, 15
    LSD, 71–72
    MDMA, 67
Harrison Narcotics Tax Act (1914), 7
health impacts
    of alcohol, 48
    of amphetamine/methamphet-
        amine, 68, 70
    of cocaine, 34, 64, 65
    of heroin, 66
    HIV/AIDS, 76–77
    of inhalants, 52, 54–55
    of LSD, 71
    of marijuana, 60–63
    of MDMA, 67–68
    of nicotine, 50–51
    of performance-enhancing drugs,
        32, 34, 55–56
    See also deaths
hemoglobin, 32–34
heroin
    abuse, 65–66
    death from, 82
    mixtures, 22
    treatment for abuse, 91
HIV/AIDS, 76–77
huffing, 53, 54

I
illegal drugs
    cost to society, 19
    cyclical nature of use, 7
    examples, 14
    in songs, 24–25
inhalants, abuse of, 52–55
International Journal of Addictions, 75
Internet, 29, 33

J
"Joe Camel," 30
Journal of Studies on Alcohol, 29
"juice," 55
"Just Say No," 8

L
Lamond, Douglas, 80, 81
Lancet, The (journal), 27

Landis, Floyd, 35
Lead on America (Law Enforcement
    Against Drugs in Our Neighbor-
    hoods), 43–44
legal drugs, 13–14
    See also medicines/medications
LSD abuse, 71–72

M
Madras, Bertha, 18
Margrethe II (queen of Denmark), 26
marijuana
    education and, 75
    effects, 60–64
    gangs and, 78
    street names, 60
    treatment for abuse, 90–91
    use by adolescents, 17, 59
    using other drugs and, 78, 79
McCarthy, Jenn, 80–81
McGwire, Mark, 35
MDMA abuse, 66–68
media coverage, 10
medicines/medications
    abuse, 56–58, 79, 82
    harmful effects, 13
    over-the-counter, 6
methamphetamine
    abuse, 68–70
    "strawberry quick," 21
    use by adolescents, 17
morphine, 6, 65
Mothers Against Drunk Driving
    (MADD), 80–81
movies, 26, 27, 29

N
National Institute on Drug Abuse
    (NIDA), 9, 46
nicotine, 13–14, 50–51
    See also cigarettes
NIDA for Teens, 46
Nixon, Richard, 7

O
Oates, Christopher, 82
"Old Camel," 30
opiates, 6, 7
    See also heroin; morphine
opioids, 57
OxyContin
    overview, 56–57
    use by adolescents, 17, 79, 82

P

pain tolerance, 34
parents, as information source, 37, 40
Partnership for a Drug-Free America, 10
peer pressure, 21, 76–77, 84–87
performance-enhancing drugs, 30, 32–36
Phoenix House, 91–92
physical dependence, 57–58, 66
Pinckard, Keith, 32
Pitt, Brad, 27, 29
potheads, 62–63
prescription drugs. *See* medicines/ medications
prevention, 8
    See also education
psychological addiction, 64
Pure Food and Drug Act (1906), 7

R

Reagan, Nancy, 8
recreational use, 16–17, 56, 66–67
regulation, 7
roids, 55
role models
    movie stars, 26, 27, 29
    older siblings, 75
    positive, 21
    royalty, 26
    sports stars, 35–36

S

SADD (Students Against Destructive Decisions), 44, 46
schools
    drug testing in, 18–20
    effect of drug use on grades, 73–75, 78
    programs in, 9, 10–11, 40–42, 44, 46
scorpion venom, 15
smoking. *See* cigarettes; nicotine
snorting, 64, 65
Sociology of Education (journal), 74
songs, 24–25
Sonoran Desert toad venom, 15
sports, 19–20, 30, 32–36
stepping-down, 58
stimulants, 34

StraightWay Team, 40–41
"strawberry quick" methamphetamine, 21
stress, 23
Substance Abuse and Mental Health Services Administration (SAMHSA) Web site, 91

T

Talbot, Travis, 43
teachers, as information source, 40–41
THC, 60, 63, 64
therapeutic committees (TCs), 90
Thompson, Kimberly M., 27
tolerances, 72
treatment
    facilities, 8, 90–92
    parts of effective, 89
    success, 88
"trips," 71

U

use
    by adolescents, 10, 17
    of cocaine, 6, 7
    cyclical nature, 7
    decline in 1980s, 9
    of marijuana, 59
    during nineteenth century, 6
    reasons for, 21–23
    recreational, 16–17, 56, 66–67
    signs of, 22

V

Ventura, Jesse, 32
Ventura, Tauny, 38–39
violence, 78–79

W

Walters, John P., 78
wasps, drug-sniffing, 16
withdrawal symptoms, 58
World Wrestling Entertainment (WWE), 32–33
wrestling, 32–33

Y

Yokota, Fumi, 27
York, Susan, 43–44
Youth to Youth International, 42, 44

ABOUT THE AUTHORS

DAMIAN KRESKE has taught biology at the high school level for the past eight years in the District of Columbia Public Schools and the Montgomery County Public Schools. He earned a biology degree from Syracuse University and a master's degree in teaching from Johns Hopkins University. He lives in Rockville, Maryland, with his wife and son.

Series introduction author **RONALD J. BROGAN** is the Bureau Chief for the New York City office of D.A.R.E. (Drug Abuse Resistance Education) America, where he trains and coordinates more than 100 New York City police officers in program-related activities. He also serves as a D.A.R.E. regional director for Oregon, Connecticut, Massachusetts, Maine, New Hampshire, New York, Rhode Island, and Vermont. In 1997, Brogan retired from the U.S. Drug Enforcement Administration (DEA), where he served as a special agent for 26 years. He holds bachelor's and master's degrees in criminal justice from the City University of New York.